IVORY

RUTHLESS CLAWS BOOK 1

MAGGIE ALABASTER

This is for all the lickable guys out there. We see you. We drool. Do you have to be so fucking delicious looking? Dammit!

TRIGGER WARNING

NOTE: Book 2 contains one non-con scene and forced sterilisation. Proceed into the series with caution.

THE GARAGE STANK of grease and fear.

Cars, or pieces of car, were spread all over the workshop. Dark stains covered the concrete floor. The smell of oil was embedded in the walls.

Terror wafted in exquisite waves from the man standing in front of me. His eyes were full of it. They had been since I walked in the door.

And I hadn't said a word.

It was Jake who spoke. Call him my second, my right hand man, whatever you want. He was one of the very few people in the world I actually trusted. In our line of work, trust was rare, but critical. Give it to the wrong person and you're fucking dead. There's no in-between.

Jake raised an eyebrow at the trembling man. He

appeared calm and cool, but his bright blue eyes pierced souls and broke down lesser people. He wouldn't just smile while he was ripping out your throat, he'd make you smile too. "We hear you've been selling artefacts."

Silas Wheeler looked from Jake to me, then to two bodyguards who accompanied us.

Ben and Kyle stared back, unblinking, matching expressions of indifference on their faces. He would get no help there. Silas already knew he was a dead man. Unless he could somehow talk his way out of trouble.

Good luck with that, I thought.

His tongue darted over his lips. I could *see* him thinking desperately. This was one of my favourite parts. When people knew they fucked up and were screwed, but they squirmed anyway. Once in a while I let them live. Usually not. Worms weren't worth the hassle. Still, I would hear him out. I was nothing if not fair.

"Some artefacts might have come my way," he admitted. "I was, um, going to let you know. I'm a busy man. You know how things are." He gave a short, high laugh. He almost, *almost* convinced himself he dug himself out of the shit.

The doubt in his eyes was both obvious and

delicious.

He continued, "I'm trying to keep this place running, more or less by myself. I thought when my nephew finished school, he would come and work for me. Ungrateful *prick* decided he's too good to dismantle cars."

Jack nodded. "It's so hard to find good help these days." To those who didn't know him, he seemed amenable, chill.

I saw the barely contained violence behind his smile and in his eyes. Lowlife slugs like Silas served their purpose, but he despised them as much as I did. People without the spine to admit when they fucked up. It wouldn't stop us from killing him if he did, but at least he might earn some respect from us first.

Silas nodded vigourously. "It really is. Young people today." He shook his head. "I don't know what the world is coming to. Am I right?" He looked at me. Apparently he hoped I would be a softer touch than Jake.

I gave him an ice cold, measured look, and he glanced away.

Hells yeah, dumbass. Nothing about me was soft. Especially not my heart. Assuming I actually had one.

"So, about those artefacts," Jake said. "The rules are the rules. You could have shut down for an hour or two. Sent word. Picked up a phone and texted. Hells, even sent up a smoke signal." His voice got more and more dangerous as he spoke.

And Silas got more and more nervous. "I *meant* to. I swear. Next time—"

"Next time," I echoed. "How many *next times* have you had already? Two? Three? We've been more than fair in giving you second chances." Several, in fact.

He served his purpose as a way to dispose of cars and cash. But I made it clear to everyone in the city of Sydney, and the rest of the state, that the sale of all magical artefacts came through me first. They weren't a common commodity, but they were fucking dangerous and I didn't want them in the hands of my enemies.

Several times, I had stopped a sale, or bought the artefact myself so I could lock it away in a safe somewhere. I knew there was a possibility people would funnel more artefacts into the area, hoping to make money from me. Whatever. I would rather have them than have those things floating around in the ether.

"You've been more than generous," Silas said. His

eyes flicked from side to side, obviously looking for a lifeline from someone. He even looked pleadingly at Kyle and Ben, but they were my men. They worked for me. Whatever I ordered them to do, they would. I trusted both almost as much as I trusted Jake. They would do nothing to help Silas.

"Yes," I agreed. "We have."

Silas looked back at Jake. He assumed the last word would come from him. That because he had a cock, he must be the one calling the shots.

So many people thought that.

They were fucking wrong.

Jake looked at me. "Ivory?"

I nodded my head. "He was useful, but he overstepped too many times. If I let him keep doing that, then others will follow." I gave Silas a brutal smile. "We can't have that."

Silas stammered, "I'll make it up to you. I can…"

"You had your chance." I nodded to Jake. "End him."

Jake grinned. "With pleasure." He gestured to Kyle and Ben. All three started to strip off their clothes and put them aside carefully.

Silas shook his head and stepped back toward the door. He put his hands up to either side of him.

"Please. I'll do anything. I swear, I won't sell any more artefacts. I just… Needed the money. *Please.*"

In a handful of moments, Jake went from a ripped, heavily tattooed naked guy in his mid-thirties, to a magnificent, snow white wolf. Kyle and Ben were a second or two behind, neither less magnificent than Jake.

Silas' face was almost as white as the three wolves who stalked around him, toying with him. "Oh gods, please no." To his credit, he hadn't pissed his pants. Yet.

Jake stepped around him lightly, as if prolonging the anticipation, or looking for the right angle to strike.

Silas murmured. The stink of fear increased a thousandfold. The smell was sweeter than fine perfume.

It was as arousing as fuck.

In the blink of an eye, Jake struck. He leaped at Silas before the man could take another step away. He clamped his jaws on the man's throat and tore it away. A shower of blood fountained from the artery in his neck. Before I could move, it rained hot blood down over my cheek and the front of my dress. It felt like someone had jerked hot cum all over me.

The feeling, the smell—I was more aroused than ever.

The guys all leaped on Silas now, tearing him apart like three dogs playing with a toy.

By the time they were done, blood added to the stains on the floors and walls. And their muzzles. Silas' head was still more or less intact. There was no point sending a message if people didn't know who we'd dispensed with.

I let the boys have a little bit of fun pushing the head around with their noses like they were playing with a ball, then cleared my throat.

"I think he's dead enough."

Jake rolled the head to my feet. I glanced down. Silas lay looking up at me with glassy eyes. I resisted the urge to soil my shoes by kicking him away. Instead I watched Jake shift back and grab a rag to wipe the blood off his face.

"Sometimes I think you have too much fun doing that." I scratched the blood on my dress with a long, black fingernail. It was going to need dry-cleaning.

He grinned. "Only when they deserve it." He tossed the rag onto a workbench, picked up his clothes and started to pull them back on.

I watched for a moment with a twinge of regret, then turned away. "This place belongs to me now.

Get the paperwork sorted. Find someone to run the place. The nephew maybe. Make it clear he's working for us, not himself." If he didn't like it, tough shit. If you screw with me, you get screwed.

"On it, boss," Jake said.

I turned back as he was doing up his pants. He scooped his shirt up off the floor. I noticed none of his clothes had blood on them. I also noticed he was taking his time putting his shirt back on.

He raised an eyebrow at me. "You smell good," he said.

I snorted. "You did that on purpose." I waved at the front of myself.

He grinned and picked up the rag he'd used to clean himself. He tossed it to me. "Would you believe it was an accident? You can clean it off if you like."

I threw it back at him and hit him in the side of the face. "That thing is dirtier than I am."

Jake caught the rag and tossed it back to the worktable. He missed. It fell on the floor with a plop.

"You don't look like you mind too much." He offered me his shirt. "You can change into this if you want."

I looked at the faded grey band T-shirt which dangled from his fingers. "I'll pass. I can change when we get back to Crimson."

He shrugged and pulled on his shirt.

While it was over his head, I *might* have taken a good long look at his abs. They looked rock hard. Every centimetre was covered in ink. A black dragon surrounded by skulls lazed across his stomach, distorted here and there with the lines of his muscles. An eagle with wings outspread soared over the dragon. A mountain rose behind it, grand like something out of a fantasy movie. I knew how many hours went into the work, but it was the body behind the art that made my breath catch.

I averted my gaze. He and I— that was a line I couldn't cross. I knew he wanted to leap over it given the chance, but it would fuck up our working relationship. How could it not? Sex changes too much. He knew that as well as I did. It didn't stop him from flirting every chance he got. And it didn't stop me from admiring him.

I watched Ben's tight, hard ass as he stepped toward the garage's small kitchen to wash his face. I immediately felt like a hypocrite for keeping Jake at arm's length. Sleeping with my bodyguard once in a while was a whole other story from sleeping with my work partner, right?

I sighed. Jake and I were different. So much more was at stake if we ruined things between us. Ben was just a smoking hot, protective distraction, that was all. Chalk and cheese. So I told myself.

I noticed neither Ben or Kyle had blood on their clothes either. Just as well. Jake got away with looking scruffy because that's who he was. As for everyone else who worked for me, I expected them to look the part. Black trousers and white shirts. Many of them toed the line by wearing a T-shirt like Jake. I let it slide because most of them were all muscle and tattoos and a girl liked to look, even if she didn't touch. Usually.

"What if this nephew isn't interested in running the place?" Jake asked. He tugged his hem into place and checked his face in the closest reflective surface. That happened to be a rear view mirror which sat on the work table. "From what Silas said, he didn't seem too keen. Want me to be persuasive?" He cocked his head and looked hopeful.

I drummed my fingernails on my thigh. "Hunt him down first. See what he has to say. We won't have too much trouble finding someone to run the place." I had a list running through my head already.

"Okay. As long as it's not me." Jake scrubbed the tip of his finger on his cheek.

I took the mirror from him and looked at my own reflection. I looked like I just killed someone, instead of *having* them killed. "I hadn't thought of that. There is no one I trust more to take care of my assets." I gave him a deadpan look.

He didn't buy it for even half a second. Fucking man knew me too well. All the more reason I should keep him close and not piss him off.

"You'd miss me too much if you relegated me to this dump," he said.

"Now I know how you feel about the place, I'll keep that in mind for the next time you give me the shits," I said.

"I'm safe then." He had a cocky look on his face. "Because that *never* happens."

I barked a laugh. "Not in the last two minutes, no."

He smirked because he knew that was total bull-shit. I let him get away with way too much.

"I know you love me," he said. His blue eyes lingered on mine for a moment, until I looked away.

How I felt, or didn't feel, didn't matter. I had to stick to that hard line, no matter what the cost.

I didn't need to look to know he was frustrated. I sensed it. It had been a bone of contention between us for so many years. We should bury it and be done with it. Only, I knew he wanted to bury his bone deep in my pussy, not the ground somewhere.

"I'm heading back to Crimson," I said, my voice cool and businesslike. "Get on to the cleanup here. Do whatever you have to do to his head to let people know what happens to them if they fuck with me."

"You should invest in a display cabinet," Jake said lightly.

His tone didn't fool me. I knew if I let him put me up on the work table and fuck me silly, he would. Part of me wanted him to. The gods knew I was horny enough. It would be safer to fuck Ben, or even Kyle. It wouldn't change anything, including Jake's feelings for me. But the workbench was dirty and so was I. The smell of fear was gone. The smell of blood faded as it dried. The excitement of having a man killed in front of me had worn off. I filed the memory in the back of my mind for another day.

"A cabinet full of heads," I mused. "That would get full pretty quickly. Cocks would take up less space."

"That depends on the cock." Jake grinned, back to his usual sardonic self.

I laughed softly. "Who do you know who has a cock the size of a head?"

His grin widened. "Well, I don't want to brag."

I rolled my eyes. I walked right into that one. But I could go one better. "Does that make you a dickhead?"

He chuckled. "Probably. I've been called worse. By you. This week."

"I don't know why you put up with me," I said honestly.

Before he could respond with another declaration of love, Ben appeared out of the shop office, a box in his hands. "Boss, I thought you should see this." The slight frown lines around his eyes were the only sign he was concerned. Considering he was usually a stony statue of absolute calm, that meant a lot. His expression softened when he looked at me.

Ugh, him too? I appreciated the admiration. It was the added complications I was worried about.

"What is it?" Jake asked, all serious now.

Ben placed the box down on the worktable. "It looks like the kind that's usually used to contain magical artefacts. I thought it best not to open it." He would know. He was orphaned as a child and raised amongst witches. Not a happy childhood, from what I could tell. On the rare occasion a witch needed to be killed, he was usually the first to volunteer. Maybe he just had a death wish. Witches were more trouble than they were worth. Luckily they tended to avoid me.

I glanced at Jake. He nodded. None of us had

magic, so there was little risk to us in opening it. Artefacts didn't tend to work by themselves.

Since there was a first time for everything, Jake opened the box carefully. Inside was a row of stones, all black but with streaks of various other colours. Two were round, two were oval-shaped and three were shaped like doughnuts. A couple were semi-precious stones.

"Wild guess: these contain magic of some kind," Jake said.

"More than likely," I agreed. There was probably a small fortune sitting inside that box. We wouldn't know how much until we had a witch look at them. "Kyle, take them to Rachel. See what she has to say about them." Rachel owned a small magic shop not far from here. She was about as reliable as a witch could be. I paid her well enough for that.

Jake snapped the box shut and handed it to Kyle. "Lucky thing we came here today. We probably put a stop to somebody's shenanigans."

I nodded. "Ben, keep searching the office and see what else you can find." If there was that much sitting out in the open, there might be more hidden away.

He nodded smartly. "Yes boss." He looked relieved I hadn't chosen him to take the artefacts to Rachel.

Given his aversion to witches, I thought it better to keep him away from her. One or the other might otherwise end up dead. That would put me in a bad mood, and no one liked to see me like that.

"Does this feel weird to you too?" Jake asked.

"Being alone with you in a garage full of chopped up cars and people?" I asked. "It's pretty weird."

He flashed a brief smile, showing a dimple in one cheek. It would be better for everyone if he wasn't so fucking attractive.

"That wasn't what I meant," he said. "We knew Silas was dealing artefacts, but seven of them, right where we could find them?"

"You think someone set him up?" I asked. "He admitted what he did."

"I know," Jake said slowly. "But it has Alastair Dagen written all over it. If he was trying to provoke you, it worked."

"Silas wasn't the smartest paranormal in the city, but why would he die just to piss me off?" I drummed my fingers on my thigh.

"Why does anyone die to piss someone else off?" Jake asked rhetorically. "Presumably he has a family they threatened. There isn't anything the Onyx Ridge pack wouldn't do to get under your skin. Or your fur. Especially Dagen."

This used to be black wolf territory, before I took it over. The only thing more cranky and aggressive than a black wolf is a white one. I wouldn't let them get in the way of what I wanted. Dagen vowed revenge, but he had yet to be more than a flea that needed to be scratched off once in a while.

"Let him try," I said. "Sooner or later, he'll realise he can't win and he'll fuck off, his tail between his legs."

"I guess you're right," Jake said. He didn't look convinced.

"Of course I'm right," I said. "When am I not right?"

"Only when the other person is wrong," he said.

"Exactly." I nodded. There were many reasons why I needed him around, including to stroke my admittedly healthy ego. "I'll see you back at Crimson."

He hesitated. "I'll send Ben with you. He can come back here after."

"I can take care of myself," I reminded him.

"If Dagen is trying to start something, I don't want you out there alone," he said firmly. "Either I go with you or Ben does. Or you wait here while I call someone else to—"

"Fine." I threw up my hands. "Ben can play nursemaid if it makes you feel better. Don't forget who is the boss around here. I own this town."

"Yes, you do," he said. "Unless you get yourself killed."

"I have no intention of dying anytime soon," I said. But his worry was infectious. It had me on edge.

THE DRIVE back to Crimson was short. I let Ben come as far as the underground car park, before I sent him and the car back to the garage. His knowledge of magical artefacts was too valuable to let him sit out for too long. I was as safe here as I was anywhere, even without him following me around. He wasn't happy about it, but unlike Jake, he didn't argue. I knew I liked him for a reason.

My heels clicked as I walked to the private elevator. This was one of only two in the building that would take me up to level ten. The only other place the elevator would stop was level six, and that was empty. Anyone who wanted a meeting with me was taken there first and checked over thoroughly before they were allowed up the rest of the way.

I stepped inside the car and rode it straight up to level ten. The moment I stepped out the sliding doors, two of my men nodded in greeting. Dressed like the rest in dark trousers and white shirts, their presence there must be Jake's doing. Sometimes the guy was fussier than a mother hen, but I couldn't help appreciating him. It was nice that someone gave a shit.

I gave them a nod in return and ignored their scrutiny. They would never give me their opinion or ask why I was covered in blood, but they were obviously curious.

I walked past the door to the main office, into the room past that. I slipped inside and closed the door behind me.

The large apartment had a stunning view of Sydney Harbour and was fitted out with all the luxuries my extensive bank accounts could buy.

I didn't actually live here, since it was common knowledge the nightclub was the cornerstone of my empire. Ivory Claw, or the Ivory Claw Pack, started here. I dropped the word 'pack' from the name of the organisation when it became obvious I would need more than white wolves to keep it running. The nightclub was one of my favourite places to be, and a base for a lot of my operations. I lived in the apartment for the first year or so, back when it was little more than a rundown building in the city with a killer view.

The moment I got a real foothold in this town, I moved somewhere else. If anyone was going to come after me in a big way, they would attack Crimson. That made living here impractical and dangerous. Only Jake and some of my security knew where I really lived. In spite of that, I spent a lot of time here, and made sure it was clean and maintained. The apartment was especially handy at times like this.

I stripped off my clothes and put them aside for my maid to deal with. They might sit there until her next day of work, but she asked no questions even when my clothes were caked with dried blood.

I grabbed my phone, checked my messages and shot off a couple of replies before I got in the shower.

The sight of Silas's blood trickling across the white tiles and down the drain was gratifying, but brief.

I washed my face and hair and I wondered about the nephew. Was it cars he wanted to avoid, or trouble? How much did he actually know about what Silas got up to? For all I knew, he was in it up to his eyeballs, but he could be as clueless as hells. If he knew nothing, it might be better to keep him out of it. I would reserve judgement until Jake found him.

I turned off the water and wrapped myself in a thick, plush towel that smelled subtly of lavender. My favourite scent after blood and fear. Okay, and testosterone.

I stepped from the bathroom straight into the walk-in wardrobe. If anyone else was to come here, they might assume I lived in the apartment. Every centimetre of my wardrobe was stuffed with something. Dresses, skirts and blouses hung on all the railings. The shoe rack was full of heels, boots and the occasional pair of flat shoes. The drawers were full of jewellery.

It was a fraction of what I owned.

I flipped off the towel, left it on the floor for the maid and pulled on a matching black lace bra and G-string.

A long, wide mirror hung off the wall. The reflection in its surface was of a woman who was fit, but not dainty, with generous hips, long legs, brown eyes and full breasts.

My white hair was almost dry already. According to my mother, it was black until the first time I shifted. When I changed back from a white wolf to a person, my hair stayed the same colour as my wolf.

Apparently it freaked the fuck out of my parents, but it never changed back. It was my father who teasingly called me Ivory, both after the pack name and because of my hair. The nickname stuck.

I brushed my hair and dug into the table beside my bed before I selected my favourite—white—vibrator. My body was still humming from watching Silas die, and being showered with his warm blood.

I walked over to the couch in front of the window and sat with my back against one of the arms, my legs stretched out in front of me. The irony of where I was wasn't lost on me. The bottom floor of Crimson was an ordinary bar. The second floor was a strip club. The third floor was a place where lovers went to have sex in front of whoever else was there at the time, like a giant orgy. The fourth and fifth floors were a brothel. Yes, the business was so lucrative it needed two floors. And yes, many of the brothel workers were male and would be only too happy, and skilled, to fuck me until I couldn't see straight. A lot of the women too.

One of the downsides to owning the place was the feeling too many people would talk if I indulged in the pleasures of Crimson. Once in a while, I ventured down to watch the stripping or the fucking, but that was all I did. Watch.

You know what they say. It's lonely at the fucking top.

I know, cry me a fucking river. I had more money than I knew what to do with, and most people did exactly what I told them when I told them to do it. Even if I told them to kill.

What can I say? Even the rich and powerful need orgasms once in a while.

I set the vibrator to a light throb and pulled the gusset of my panties aside. I sat back a little more and rubbed the thrumming vibrator over my clit, just lightly at first. It sent a delicious shiver of pleasure right to my core.

I let it ghost over my clit and folds for a minute or two, until my thighs started to quiver and my pussy was wet.

I parted my legs further and slid the silicone dick slowly inside myself. The clit stimulator hummed against my sensitive nub. I quivered a little more.

Slowly I slid the toy out, and in again, teasing my clit and my g spot. I slipped my other hand inside my bra and lightly ran the tip of my finger around and over my nipple.

I was already panting through my nose. I closed my eyes and turned the vibrator up to a heavier throb.

I slid it in and out faster, then stopped to spoil my clit for a minute or two.

I was so engrossed in pleasuring myself, I almost missed the sound of the door opening and closing. I managed to keep myself from jumping out of my skin, but my eyes flew open.

Jake stood leaning against the closed door, arms crossed over his chest. He watched me with one raised eyebrow. And a tent in his pants.

Instead of stopping and acting like I did something wrong, I locked my eyes with his and kept working my clit and my nipple. I watched him watching me as I came, moaning and bucking against the humming vibrator.

I leaned my head against the arm of the couch while I came down, then slid the toy out. I drew my gusset back into place and put the vibrator down on the coffee table next to the couch.

"Shouldn't you be on cleanup?" I stood as though he hadn't seen me pleasuring myself and I wasn't dressed in a bra and panties.

"Clean up." He shrugged one shoulder and walked over to the coffee table. He picked up the vibrator and licked his tongue down the wand, which was probably still warm and slick from being inside me.

While I shook my head at him, he went on licking all the way around it, smiling the whole time. Finally, he put it back down on the table.

"There. All clean. Delicious too." He glanced at me up and down, obviously not just referring to the taste of me.

"I knew someday you would be useful for something." I made a face at him but at the same time I tried to keep a smile back. No one else I ever met would do something like that. No one else would get away with it either, and he knew it. Not even Ben. Sometimes we danced *way* too close to that line.

He gave me an ironic bow. "I live to serve."

I snorted. "Sure you do. What was so important you had to come in here without knocking?"

"I did knock," he said. "When I didn't hear an answer, I thought you might need help. Turns out I was right."

I rolled my eyes and waved at him to get on with whatever he actually came here for. While he spoke, I headed into my wardrobe and grabbed a blouse.

"I thought you would want to know I found the nephew." He at least had the sense to stay out of the wardrobe.

"Okay." I pulled on the blouse and did the buttons up. I took a second to contemplate Jake's timing. He couldn't have known what I was doing, and I believed him when he said he knocked. I was distracted. Too distracted. He could have been an assassin.

He also could have turned and crept back out the door. If he waited five minutes, or ten, I would have been done. If he was anyone else, I would be sure his body was floating in Sydney Harbour before night fell. Instead, I realised I *liked* seeing him watch me.

And that terrified me. I could not, would not walk across that line, no matter how much I wanted to. In the long time we've known each other, there were other men, apart from Ben. Quite a few of them. None of them ever meant anything, and Jake never seemed to mind. When the dust settled, I always circled back to him. It was like a dance, but only he and I knew the steps or the song that went with it.

"Where is he?" I asked. I took a skirt off the hanger and stepped into it. As I slid up the zipper, a tiny part of me acknowledged that I wished Jake was sliding it *down*.

I pressed my feet into a pair of black heels and walked back out of the wardrobe. In heels I was almost as tall as Jake, which is why I wore them.

"I'm not sure where he is right now," Jake admitted. "But I know where he's going to be tonight."

"It's not like you to be so cryptic." I stepped over to the kitchen and turned on the coffee machine.

"Isn't it? I'll have to work harder at that." He went to the cupboard and pulled out two coffee mugs.

"How about you don't," I said. "I don't like to be kept guessing all the time. But you already know that about me." What *didn't* he know about me? We had both seen each other naked more times than I could count. Hazards of being a shifter. He knew most of my secrets. Those he didn't know probably weren't worth knowing. Or at least weren't worth remembering.

"I do know that," he agreed. "I also know you can be patient when you need to be."

"Yeah." I waited and worked in the shadows for years before I was able to strike back at Barnaby Dagen and the whole Onyx Ridge pack. "It's been a while since I've needed to be patient. These days I can pay people to be patient for me."

He chuckled and made us both coffee. "Who says money can't buy happiness?" He looked at me over the rim of his mug. His thoughts were as transparent as the window behind him. What was the point of money if he couldn't have the one thing he really desired?

I looked away.

"El—" He was one of the very few people who knew my real name, much less got away with using even a part of it.

I shook my head. "What about this nephew?"

"Elodie… " In the corner of my eye, I saw him reach out a hand towards me, then lower it again. He sighed. "He'll be here tonight. At Crimson."

I turned back in surprise. My mouth formed an O. "Silas must've been in more debt than we realised."

"It's all on his computer. I forwarded you a copy. He was in a shit load of debt to Alastair Dagen." He gulped his coffee and made a face at how hot it was.

"It must be significant if this nephew would come here tonight." I blew on the top of my coffee gently. "It's not something anyone should do lightly."

"It's something someone would have to be desperate to do," Jake agreed gently.

I glanced down at the dark hardwood floor. "Yeah. I assume his alternative would be to be in debt to Dagen for the rest of his life?"

"And the lives of his children," Jake agreed.

"It's that much?" I asked.

"Not for you or me, but if all you have in the world is a chop shop, then it would be virtually impossible to pay all of that back." Jake sipped his coffee, which must have cooled enough by now.

I nodded. I remembered the days of living hand to mouth all too well. Sometimes it didn't matter how hard you worked, you would still always live that way. I was one of the lucky ones. Or one of the ruthless ones. Maybe both.

"I guess I know what I'll be doing tonight," I said. "You want to tag along?"

"I was going to wash my hair, but that sounds like a much better idea." He grinned.

"Good." Only now I was picturing Jake naked, with water and suds sliding down his body. I pushed away the thought. I needed to focus on more important things, like what I was going to wear tonight.

Jake must have read my mind, because he asked, "Do I have to wear a suit?" His lips curled at the idea.

"When you put it that way, yes," I said. "This is a Crimson event. You should have a suit ready for it."

"I do," he said. "But usually something comes up every time we plan anything like this. Last time it was that stupid motherfucker who tried to pass himself off as one of us."

"Right. He ended up part of the concrete in the

foundations of one of our buildings, didn't he?" I asked. I couldn't possibly remember the way we disposed of everyone.

"That's the guy." Jake gulped down the last of his coffee and put his mug on the counter top. "The time before that it was the Onyx Ridge pack stirring up trouble."

"And this time we need to go because this nephew of Silas' is deep in debt to Dagen. It's never a dull moment around here." Once in a while, I could use a little boredom. Just for an hour or two.

"Run the biggest criminal organisation in the state they said. It'll be fun they said," Jake joked.

I laughed. "Who said that? I only did this because the Onyx Ridge pack murdered my parents and took over what they built. All I did was take it back."

Of course, Jake knew all of that. He smiled sympathetically. "You could have had a nice, quiet life. Become a teacher or a police officer."

I laughed harder than before. "Police officer? Wouldn't that be ironic?" I had a bunch of them on my payroll. The rest were oblivious. Or pretended to be.

Jake chuckled. "I would let you arrest me."

And we were back to that again.

"I don't think I could arrest you," I said.

"Because I'm so handsome and charming you would let me get away with anything?" he asked teasingly.

"No. Because you're an arrogant motherfucker. I'd shoot you on sight and save myself the trouble." I swallowed my last mouthful of coffee and put my mug down beside his.

He grunted. "You're a hard woman, El."

"I know," I said. "That's why I should probably fire you and make you go off and find a nice girl and a decent, legitimate job."

He barked a laugh. "You like me too much to inflict that kind of torture on me."

That was half the problem. I should push him away harder than I did. He deserved better than to pine after me and hope to once in a while walk in on me with a vibrator in my pussy. He should meet someone. She didn't have to be a *nice* girl, if that wasn't what he was into.

What the shit was I thinking? If he liked *nice* girls, he wouldn't be into me. If I wasn't such a selfish asshole, I would force him to stay away from me. The truth was, I liked having him around.

"We should start getting ready for tonight."

3

"ARE YOU READY YET?"

This time I heard Jake knock so I was ready for him to enter. I wasn't ready for how stinking hot he looked.

He wore a perfectly tailored dark suit that fit so well it could have been painted on. Under that was a crisp white shirt and crimson and red striped tie. He had just enough scruff on his chin for that designer badass look. Although most of his tattoos were covered, the ones on his wrists peeked out from his sleeves, hinting at what else was there.

While I drank in the sight of him, he did the same to me.

He let out a soft, low wolf whistle, no pun intended. Okay, yes it was.

"No one else will be looking at anyone but you," he said smoothly.

"What? In this old thing?" I put my hands out to either side and did a turn, showing off my long, white shimmering gown. The neckline plunged low enough to show a barely decent amount of cleavage. The back plunged even lower. It covered my ass by about a millimetre. Just below the base of my neck was a tattoo of a wolf's head, surrounded by flowers. I liked to be part wolf, even in human form.

A split in the side of the dress showed a lot of thigh. White stilettos completed the outfit.

"If you wore shorts, a T-shirt and thongs on your feet, people would still only look at you," he said.

I laughed softly. "Is that a challenge?"

He chuckled. "Only if I thought you'd take me up on it. If we're going to go there, let's go one more. I dare you to go naked."

I leaned over towards the mirror to apply my lipstick. "Are you hoping I'll say yes so you can go naked too?"

He stood behind me so I could see his reflection grin. "When have I ever had trouble being naked?"

"Never," I agreed. "But that's not the impression we need to make tonight."

He snapped his fingers. "Okay. We'll save that for another night."

I grabbed a tissue and dabbed my lipstick."How many do we have coming to our little event?"

"Attendees or... Special guests?" he asked carefully. He watched my expression in the mirror.

I made a face at him. "Both."

He nodded. "About two hundred attendees. Eleven special guests."

I knitted my eyebrows. "That many?"

Jake shrugged. "Times are tight."

"I guess so." I straightened up and turned to face him. "We shouldn't be fashionably late. They'll start without us."

"They wouldn't dare. I told them you're coming." He put a hand on my arm, just above my elbow. "Are you okay? I know these things bring back memories." His eyes bore into mine like he was trying to see into my soul.

"It wasn't all bad memories," I reminded him. "I'll be fine. We just have to focus on what we have to do tonight. This is all about the nephew."

Jake nodded slowly. "In that case, can I ask another question?"

I arched one shapely eyebrow at him. "Can I stop you?"

He looked thoughtful. "Technically, yes, but you'd have to have me killed. I need to know the answer to this. It's important."

He made me nervous, until he said, "How the fuck is your gown staying on?" He looked at me sideways, then the other way.

"Magic," I said jokingly. The truth was, my dressmaker was a genius. He managed to make clothes that looked incredible, and stayed in place with stitching in just the right place on my shoulders or waist.

"Is it sticky tape?" he asked. "Can I find out?"

I patted him lightly on the chest. "It's not sticky tape, and no you can't. Come on, we'll be late." And if we didn't leave now, I might change my mind about crossing the line with him. Besides, my gown cost six thousand dollars. I should at least wear it for an hour or two.

"Anyone who comes after you is late." Jake opened the door and waved for me to step through first.

"On the contrary." I swept through the doorway and into the corridor. "Anyone who comes after me is a gentleman."

He chuckled. "Touché. For the record, I would never do that."

I looked at him over my shoulder. "I know." I pressed my hand on the palm pad beside the elevator door. It scanned my hand and turned green. The elevator doors slid open.

I pressed the button for the sixth floor and the doors slid shut. Neither of us minded enclosed spaces, but we both knew if anyone was going to attack Crimson, this would be a shit place to get stuck.

Fortunately, we reached the sixth floor without incident. We got out and crossed to the other elevator which led down into the rest of the night club.

Jake used his palm this time on the palm pad, and pressed the button for the second floor.

The elevator doors slid open to a scene of bustle and noise. This floor was usually reserved for the strip club, but tonight a sign read 'closed for private event' hung on a velvet rope in front of the doorway.

Entry to this event was exclusive and by invitation only.

One of the security men on the door unclipped the rope before we even got there and stepped aside. He gave us both a respectful, but slightly anxious nod, before looking me up and down appreciatively.

I ignored him and stepped past.

Jake placed his hand on my lower back. His demeanour changed immediately, visibly. He went from the chill, amenable, even approachable guy, to the cold, hard alpha male of the Ivory Claw Pack. One of his fingers rested just below where the back of my dress ended, under the shimmery fabric, his fingertip on my ass.

Typical alpha male possessive shit. It was a move everyone would expect. That was one reason I allowed it. That and I liked the way it felt.

I lifted my chin and scanned the room, my ice queen persona firmly in place.

Everyone here was dressed in formal, expensive-as-fuck suits and dresses. Many of them were wolves, but I caught a scent of what might be a tiger or some other big cat.

All eyes were on Jake and I as we walked through the room to the chairs at the front reserved for us.

I heard somebody mutter, "Ice bitch," and the muscles around my cheeks twitched. If there was anything that would get you dead around me, it was using the word bitch as if it was a bad thing. I wasn't oblivious to the nickname, but whoever used it was either bold or stupid.

Jake's finger pressed into my ass cheek, letting

me know he'd heard it too. He would deal with it later.

"Ahhh, how nice of you to grace us with your presence." Alastair Dagen stepped away from the group he was talking to and gave me a sardonic bow. He looked me over like he wasn't sure if he wanted to fuck me or kill me. Maybe both. I don't think he cared which order those events took place. He was a sadistic fucker who seemed to get worse by the year.

"The infamous El— Ivory, and her favourite lapdog." His apparent misstep was purposeful, to remind me he also knew my real name, and exactly where I came from. "Have you come to buy? Or sell?"

I didn't give him the satisfaction of getting angry. The virgin auction was a part of my past, and the way I got to where I was now. I reminded myself it wasn't his fault I was that desperate. It was his parents who murdered mine and took everything they built. In retaliation, I had his parents killed. I understood his burning need for revenge, because I had lived it for so many years. Unfortunately for him, I had no intention of letting him be successful.

I laughed. "I could ask the same of you. If you're so hard up for a fuck, I'd be happy to let you have a free hour in the brothel." And if, or rather, when he raised a hand against my staff, I would have an excuse to cut his throat.

He chuckled, but his dark brown eyes narrowed. "Always such a charming host. That's why I had to accept your invitation to be here this evening. Who else in town holds a better party? Besides, it gives me a chance to decide what decor I'm going to replace when I own this place."

I would have retorted that him owning Crimson would be over my dead body, but that was the point. *Good luck with that, assprick.*

"Would you like a drink?" Jake asked him. "I hear the whiskey is especially fine. On the house, of course."

Alastair curled his lip at Jake. "You first, lapdog."

As wolves, none of us could eat or drink anything that was toxic to canines of any kind. That included alcohol and chocolate. At least we could drink coffee and tea, although in smaller doses than humans or other paranormals. It was a small price to pay for being a wolf.

Jake turned to me. "I'm starting to think he doesn't like me." Truthfully, Alastair had as much reason to like Jake as he had to like me. He was by my side every step of my way back from beaten down omega to alpha female and head of an organisation that dwarfed the scope of the Dagen pack and anything my parents did.

"Actually," Alastair said, "I pity you. You don't seem to have any more ambition than to be sidekick to this bitch."

It took every drop of willpower not to scratch his eyes out with my nails. He was trying to get to me. I couldn't let him. That was what he wanted. If I attacked him, he would have an excuse to shift and tear me apart. He was unlikely to be the only black wolf here tonight.

"Jake, I think we need to *vet* the guest list better for next year," I said coldly. The truth was, I made sure he was invited so I could keep an eye on him. Alastair Dagen was not the kind of man you turned your back on. Ever. If I could kill him without provoking the Onyx Ridge pack, I would do it and get it over with. Although, then the pack would just choose a replacement and I would have to start all over again with some other asshole. It would be easier to annihilate them, which I would do if I could. Some of the black wolves were actually useful, and paranormalkind in general didn't look too kindly on genocide. The fact the black wolves had tried so hard to annihilate the white twenty years ago wouldn't excuse me from doing the opposite now.

Even I had to follow some laws, though they chafed.

Alastair gave me a smug look, like he was certain I wouldn't be calling the shots this time next year.

In spite of myself, I got a shiver down my spine. I didn't know where or when, yet, but he would make a move against me. It was as inevitable as the sun rising tomorrow. His failure was just as inevitable.

"We should take our seats," Alastair said as though I was keeping him from his. "This should be interesting." He gave me a last look like he was peeling my dress off my body, then my skin under that. He turned and walked away leaving me feeling naked and dirty.

"I'm starting to think I should have taken you up on the challenge of wearing shorts and a T-shirt," I whispered to Jake.

"Don't let him get to you." He led me over to our chairs and we sat, one of his hands on one of mine. It was more than a possessive gesture. It was an offer of comfort in spite of me managing to hide how rattled I was from everyone but Jake.

"That's what he wants."

"He wants a lot more than that," I said softly.

"He'd like nothing more than to see me on my knees."

"Want me to kill him for you?" One of Jake's eyebrows twitched, the only visible sign of his amusement. He was as good at containing his emotions as I was. Curious how he never attracted nicknames like Ice Bitch. What would they call him anyway? Ice Dog sounded like a rapper. He would probably enjoy that nickname. Maybe Ice Hole. No, he would like that too.

"I'd love that," I said. "I wish we could."

Just as I said that, the house lights went down, and the stage was illuminated. The men and women who attended the auction in the hope of buying a virgin to deflower fell quiet.

The auctioneer led out the line of eleven 'special guests,' as Jake called them. Eleven virgins who, for whatever reason, were so desperate for money, the only thing they had left to sell was themselves.

I vividly recalled stepping out on that stage nine years ago. I was barely eighteen, the minimum age allowed here. Other auctions allowed for younger virgins, but Crimson, or Black Gold as it was known back then, kept itself to a higher standard. When I bought the place, I kept that standard. I might be a killer, but I didn't sell children.

The stage then was older than the one in its place today, worn, shabby. The whole building was tired and falling into disarray. It was just another property belonging to the Onyx Ridge pack in general and the Dagen family in particular. One they paid little attention and even less money, to. It was me who saw the potential in this place.

The moment I stepped out onto the stage in just my underwear, I decided if I made enough money from selling myself, I would buy the place. Make it something special.

I recalled the feeling of fear and vulnerability. I saw it on the faces of the virgins on the stage now. They had no idea who would bid on them, who would win and what they would do with them afterwards. The money would change their lives, but would it be worth it?

"The nephew is the last one," Jake whispered, his mouth right next to my ear. "Guy with dark blond hair. Cooper Wheeler."

I hadn't really looked, but I looked now. Only through sheer strength of will did I keep my jaw from dropping.

You know when someone describes a guy as lickable? Well, I wanted to lick my way down this guy's entire fucking body. His abs must feel like solid rock.

I didn't know which I wanted to touch him with more, my fingers or my tongue. Probably both.

Even with boxers on, his cock was obviously huge. He turned around slowly when the auctioneer told him to. Of course he had the most perfect, smackable ass I ever saw. His hair was tousled, like he'd just pulled off his shirt. A piercing in his left eyebrow caught the overhead lights for a moment.

My core throbbed. I was definitely going to need to change my panties.

And that was before he looked at me with his hazel eyes and smiled.

Holy.

Fucking.

Gods.

"You're staring," Jake said.

I blinked. "What? Oh." Alastair Dagen could have burnt the whole place down and I wouldn't have noticed. "That guy is Silas Wheeler's nephew?" He definitely didn't get his looks from his uncle.

I tried to remind the inner, panting orgasm-maker that was connected to my suddenly very hungry pussy, that Cooper was little more than a kid. Eight or nine years younger than me. The age gap was about the same as it was between Jake and I, but Cooper was probably innocent. And I certainly wasn't. He certainly fucking wouldn't be when I was done with him.

"Should I write a blank cheque right now?" Jake asked teasingly.

I realised I hadn't looked away from Cooper. Worse than that, I actually smiled back at him. Yeah, apparently the ice queen cracks for a pretty face and hot body.

"I mean, someone has to help him out of debt." Was I actually blushing? *Fucking hells*, I told myself. *Pull yourself together, woman.* I was unable to look at a trinket and walk away without buying it, and this guy was more than a trinket. He was a tasty-ass snack straight from the oven.

I swallowed hard.

I just wanted to help the kid. We *had* killed his uncle. And if Silas was in trouble with the Onyx Ridge pack, then this was the best way to get Cooper out of the hands of an asshole like Alistair Dagen.

At least, that's what I told myself.

"Your wish is my command," Jake said softly. "Any others up there you want?"

There were others up there? Oh yeah, ten of them. I forgot they existed for a few moments there. They all paled in comparison to Cooper.

"No, you?" I asked. Most of the virgins were girls.

All of them were pretty, with perfect, lush bodies and soft curves. If Jake wanted to take one of them home, I would support that. I would hate her and want to scratch her eyes out, but I would do nothing to stop him. Just as he would support me if I desperately wanted to lick Cooper from head to foot.

Jake shook his head. "None of them look like my type. I prefer a woman with fire. Who doesn't mind burning the world down around her."

"That sounds dangerous," I said lightly.

"It is," he agreed. "I'm a masochist. But I also want you to be happy."

"I want that for you too," I said.

"I know you do." He squeezed my hand lightly. "I'm willing to wait until you realise we both want the same thing. In the meantime, let me buy you a present." When the time came to bid for Cooper's virginity, Jake raised his hand.

4

Cooper stared around my apartment with wide eyes. He was dressed now, in worn blue jeans and a black T-shirt that moulded to his body. Somehow he looked sexier than when he only wore boxers.

"This is where you live?" he asked. He looked like he didn't quite believe he was here.

I didn't quite believe it myself.

Jake questioned the wisdom of bringing Cooper up here in the first place, but he and I had some talking to do.

"Not exactly," I said. "I crash here sometimes. Jake too. There's a couple of spare bedrooms. It comes in useful." I sat down on the couch and crossed my legs, letting the split in my dress fall open to show most of my thigh.

"Right." Cooper gawked at the view outside the window for a while longer, then sat down on the couch near me. He glanced at my exposed leg and swallowed hard.

Jake flopped into a chair opposite us. His tie hung loose around his neck. The first few buttons on his shirt were undone, showing a glimpse of his chest. To anyone else, he might seem relaxed, unwound after a long night of schmoozing. I knew he would shift and rip Cooper's throat out in a heartbeat if he thought it was necessary. Hopefully it wouldn't come to that.

A jar of red cherries he'd snagged from the bar hung loosely from his fingers. Smartass.

"So—" Cooper said awkwardly.

"There's a few things you should know," I started. I nodded towards Jake. He was better at this shit than I was.

Before Jake could speak, Cooper said, "You killed my uncle."

Things went to a whole new level of awkward.

Jake cleared his throat and shrugged one shoulder. "Yep."

"Okay." Cooper nodded, his brow creased slightly. "If you hadn't, the Dagens would have. I told him he was gonna get in too much shit someday. He wouldn't listen. I even told him he should come to you for help."

He looked regretful. "They threatened him, I guess."

"That sounds like Dagen," I said. And me. Threats were a part of the job. "And now you have enough money to pay Dagen off. I don't expect anything in return."

No, that wasn't exactly true. I didn't expect him to fuck me just because we won the auction. When it came to sex, I was all about consent. I would call on him for a favour in return for us helping him out of the shit, but he didn't need to know that yet.

"I think I have a few hundred thousand left after I pay them off." Cooper smiled slowly. "Was that, like, some sort of record? What you paid, I mean."

Jake chuckled.

"It was high, but the record is higher," I said gently.

"Oh." Cooper's face fell. "What is the record?"

I took a few beats before I responded. "It's one point six million. Held by me."

Silence fell for a moment before Cooper broke it. "Oh," he said again. His eyebrows shot up. "You…"

"Sold my virginity for one point six million dollars, yes," I said. "One point two is a lot higher than most." I don't know who else was bidding, but I suspected they were bidding on behalf of Alistair Dagen. The moment anyone was aware of Jake's bidding, they would have wanted to push up the price, just to piss me off. Whatever, that amount of money was spare change.

"Okay," Cooper said. He looked from me to Jake and back again. "You two are… Together?"

I glanced at Jake as his expression tightened slightly. I would have missed it if I wasn't watching.

I looked back at Cooper. "No, not exactly," I said. "Just once, before we worked together." Before I drew that line.

Jake unscrewed the lid of the jar, pulled out a cherry and popped it in his mouth. "Best one point six million I ever spent."

That clearly took Cooper by surprise. "You bought… You paid… I…"

"It was a long time ago," I said quickly. I would never stop being grateful to Jake for making that winning bid. It was Alistair Dagen's father he bid against. If Dagen won, the night I lost my virginity would have been the last night I lived. I knew that with absolute certainty. What better way to finalise the conquest of the Ivory Claw Pack than the rape and murder of the daughter of the last Alphas on the tenth anniversary of their death? Even if I survived that night, they would have married me off to Alistair or someone equally horrible.

"Do you want to run your uncle's garage?" Jake asked bluntly. "Ivory owns it now, but maybe you could make some kind of arrangement."

Cooper shook his head. "Gods no. You're welcome to the place. I don't want any part of it. I would rather work for you."

Now I was the one taken by surprise. "For us? You know what we do, right?"

Cooper looked like he was ready to jump up and down in his seat. "I know you don't take shit from anyone. I know no one dares to cross you. You're also smoking hot."

Jake tossed a cherry up in the air and caught it in his mouth. "Thank you." He chewed and wiggled his eyebrows.

Cooper grinned. "I mean, you are too, but I meant her." He nodded towards me.

"Of course you did," Jake said around his mouthful. "You're right, she is."

The smell of testosterone in the room was next level. It was sweeter than a drug.

"I would kill for you," Cooper told me softly.

His tone gave me a delicious chill down my

spine. Call it an asset or a flaw, but us white wolves loved to kill. He was a white wolf too, I could smell it on him the moment I saw him. Nothing was more sensual. If I could bottle it and sell it like perfume, I'd be more ridiculously rich than I already was.

"I'm sure we can find an opening somewhere," I said. "I could always use more bodyguards when Jake goes all nursemaid on me."

Jake snorted. "I'll bet you can find an opening for him." He was teasing, but there was an edge of envy in his voice. He knew I wanted to fuck Cooper like an itch I needed to scratch. It was different from my feelings for Jake. More carnal.

Cooper actually blushed, bless him and his hot little fucking ass. He was too adorable for his own good. And probably mine.

"You really want to work with the people that killed your uncle?" I asked. "If it was me, I would want revenge."

Cooper shrugged. "Like I said, he had it coming. I... Kinda wish I'd been there to see it."

Fuck, there was a darkness in this guy. It turned me on so hard I wanted to come just listening to the sound of his voice.

"It was pretty awesome," Jake remarked."He ejaculated his blood all over Ivory."

"That was Jake's fault," I said immediately.

"Don't pretend like you hated it," Jake said. To Cooper he said, "If she wasn't a wolf, she would be a vampire. She has a thing for hot blood."

"I do not," I protested. "I just like how it feels and smells. And tastes. Besides, there's no such thing as vampires."

Jake gave Cooper a knowing nod.

Cooper grinned.

Boys.

It could be a good thing if they got along with each other. I had a feeling Cooper might make himself indispensable.

Jake stretched and put the empty jar down on the table. "I'm going to get some sleep. You kids have a good time."

I smiled and nodded. "Good night."

He gave Cooper a warning look which clearly said, 'If you fuck with her, you'll fuck with me,' then disappeared into the spare room he preferred.

I found myself gazing into Cooper's pretty, hazel eyes. "You have enough money now to make a good start in life. A legal one. Isn't that why you took part in the auction?"

"I wanted the money to pay off my uncle's debts and to put myself through university." Cooper glanced in the direction Jake went. He suddenly looked nervous, but excited at the same time.

Yeah, so was I.

"Oh? What are you studying?" I managed to keep my voice even.

"Visual arts," Jake called out from the spare room. Obviously he wanted to let Cooper know he was still listening, and that he'd been thoroughly vetted by us. Jake would have done an extensive background check before he even mentioned the auction to me.

"You're an artist?" I asked. "Jake has a PhD in eavesdropping."

"Just call me Doctor Claw," Jake said.

Cooper and I both laughed.

"I like to paint and draw," Cooper said. "Traditionally and digitally. I wanted to get into graphic design."

"Past tense?" I asked. "You don't anymore?"

Cooper took a full minute to respond. "I think there's a bigger world out there. More to life than staring at a screen or canvas. I can still do all that as a hobby."

I nodded slowly, then rose and moved to look out the window. "This life is not an easy choice to make. It's not an easy one to live. It looks like fun in the movies and on TV, but the reality is a lot more...

Sometimes boring. Sometimes bloody. Do you really want to spend the rest of your life looking over your shoulder? Because you will. You won't even notice you're doing it. You'll find yourself lying to everyone you ever knew. Before you know it, the only friends you have are people you work with. They are the only ones who know what we do. They're the only ones who don't care."

Cooper stepped up behind me and put his hands lightly on my shoulders. "You make that sound more and more appealing."

His touch made it harder to think.

"I know I paid for your virginity, but I don't expect you to give it to me," I said, my voice huskier than I intended. "I don't want anything you're not prepared to give willingly."

"I want to give it to you," he said softly. He leaned in and kissed the side of my neck.

Just that light touch made my knees turn to jelly. I tilted my head to the side to give him better access.

He must have taken that as encouragement, because he kissed his way from my neck, down the top of my shoulders. He peeled one side of my dress off my shoulder, then the other. It slid down my body and pooled on the floor at my feet.

I stepped out of it, and turned to face him, wearing only white, lace panties.

He gulped. "Holy shit. You're gorgeous."

I slid my hands up the front of his shirt. I was right about his abs being as hard as a rock. I ran my fingertips up every defined muscle, pushing his shirt up as I went. When it reached the top of his chest, I pulled it out far enough to push it over his head and onto the floor.

"You're the gorgeous one." I leaned forward to run the tip of my tongue over his taut chest. "How are you possibly a virgin?" Honestly, I didn't give a shit if it was false advertising. He was just so incredibly fuckable.

"I was saving myself for you," he said smoothly.

I snorted. "Word of advice. Don't try to bullshit a bullshitter." The flattery was nice, but there must be a real reason.

"I was busy studying and working out," he admitted. "And most of the girls I know were… I don't know. Girls. I was always more into *women*."

"That's better," I said approvingly. "Never lie to me and I will never lie to you. We save that for people who try to fuck with us."

"Us." He grinned. "I like the sound of that. Does that mean I'm in?"

"Oh, you're in." I put my hands around his neck and pulled his face down to kiss him.

His hands went to my breasts. Lightly at first. Then with more confidence. He rubbed his wide palms against my nipples. "I never imagined anyone could feel so good."

Fireworks went off the moment our lips met. Flashes, wheels, cascades, the works.

Okay, maybe the cascade was in my panties.

"I want you," I said between kisses.

"I want you too," he replied.

I broke off the kiss, took his hand and led him towards my bedroom. I glanced at the door to the spare room. It was ajar. No doubt Jake was listening, still on duty against the chance Cooper might attack me. The security outside the door would be listening for the same thing.

I wasn't oblivious to the possibility, but I intended to enjoy the rest of the night. I could take care of myself anyway. Someone in my position would be stupid not to learn how, in person form as well as wolf.

I pushed Cooper down on my bed on his back and straddled his thighs. I undid the button on his jeans and slid the zipper down slowly. He lifted his hips and let me slide down jeans and boxers until his erection was free.

Just as I guessed during the auction, his cock was big. Enough for a good handful. Or mouthful.

I shimmied down until my shoulder was on his thigh, then lightly ran the tip of my tongue from his balls to the bead of precum on the end of his dick.

He moaned and his hips twitched. "Wow. That feels so..."

I smiled. "It's just the beginning." I licked him thoroughly, all the way around his length like Jake had with my vibrator. Cooper was quivering, and his cock rock hard by the time I took him into my mouth. At first, my lips barely touched him. I teased him with my tongue for a few moments before I began to suck.

"Holy fuck," he breathed. "I'm not gonna last long if you keep doing that."

I lifted my mouth off him to say, "Then don't. We have all night." A guy like him might be addictive. I lowered my mouth and went back to sucking while I slid my fingers up his legs and started to trace circles around his balls.

He groaned and started to pant through his nose. His hips moved, thrusting his cock harder and faster into my mouth.

"Ivory…" Whatever he was trying to say was cut off by him coming. He let off a half grunt, half shout and thrust furiously, before he stilled and ground up into me. "Gods, gods, holy fuck."

The only thing better than blood was the feel, smell and taste of hot cum. When it flooded into my mouth, I drank it like it was nectar, sucking until I got the last drop. Only when he sagged did I finally let him go.

"Wow. I thought I knew the meaning of mind blowing." He stared at me with wide eyes full of admiration and awe.

I smiled and crept up his body, stopping every few moments to lick here, run my fingers there. "You ain't seen nothing yet."

"I have a feeling you're right." His cock was already starting to twitch back to life.

I straddled his thighs again and thoroughly indulged my need to lick his abs and chest. "You realise you're absolutely, insanely gorgeous, right?" I said between licks. "I think you belong with us, because being this hot is probably illegal anyway."

He chuckled. "I was going to say the same thing to you." Without warning, he rolled us over so he lay on top of me. "My turn."

He gave the same careful attention I had given

him to my breasts. In spite of me trying to put them in his path every couple of minutes, he left my nipples until last. When his tongue finally grazed across my aroused-as-fuck peaks, I let out a half moan, half pant.

"You taste delicious." He clamped his lips around my nipple and started to suck.

I had absolutely no words by now. All I could do was push my chest forward, pressing my breasts into his face.

His hands slipped out between my legs.

Eagerly, I opened them for him. I grabbed his fingers and guided them to my clit. I heard him swallow, then he tentatively ran his fingers over and around my nub and folds.

I let out a little whimper.

He froze. "I'm sorry did I..."

"Oh, gods, Cooper," I breathlessly. "Don't stop. That's perfect. You're perfect."

He sighed with relief and went back to doing what he was doing so well. He rubbed my clit and slipped a finger inside me. "Wow. You're so wet. That is so fucking hot." He sounded like he just discovered potatoes were edible if you cook them. I mean, that was one hell of a discovery. So, apparently, was this.

"That's because I want you so fucking bad," I said.

I was on the edge of coming. How I held out this long, I don't know. I slid my hand down and ran it over his cock. He was already half hard again before I touched him, but he was fully erect a moment or two later.

"Can I—" He traced a finger around the entrance to my pussy.

"I'm going to scream if you don't," I said. I wanted all of him inside me and I wanted it now.

He pulled his hand away and knelt between my legs.

I put my hand between us and guided his cock to my pussy.

When I took my hand away, he locked his eyes on mine and pressed the tip of his cock into me. His eyes widened.

I pressed my hands onto his tight little ass, lightly dug in my fingernails and pushed him down encouragingly.

Slowly, as though he wanted to record every moment of this in his memory, he slid down slowly, deeper and deeper until he was finally all the way inside me.

"Holy fucking hells," he said softly. "I thought your mouth was amazing. But this…"

I guessed he liked my pussy.

Taking his time, he started to slide in and out of me, making every moment last.

"You feel so good," I said. Whoever said size doesn't matter didn't have a cock like Cooper's deep inside them. The more he thrust, the closer I got to my own orgasm.

Supporting most of his weight on his hands and arms, he thrust harder, a little faster each time.

I moaned. "I'm going to come."

"I want to hear you," he said. "I want to hear you come."

I had briefly forgotten this was his first time. That he had probably never made a woman come before. I couldn't have stopped the cry that slipped out between my lips if I'd wanted to. But I didn't. I wanted to scream for him, to make this memorable.

"Coop." The shortened version of his name was all I could get out before I came, moaning and bucking so his cock rubbed my G spot and my clit, alternating as he thrust. My back arched and I all but screamed as I came, the orgasm slamming into me like a thunderous wall of pleasure.

"Ivory." He thrust hard, deep, frantic. His cry when he came again was no less intense than mine. His breath came in ragged gasps. "Fuck... Yeah... Fuck."

Finally, he sagged and rolled so he lay beside me while we both caught our breath.

"That was," pant, "absolutely," pant, "incredible."

I smiled over at him. "You are everything I hoped you would be. And more. Are you sure that was your first time?"

He grinned. "It was. But not the last." He leaned forward to claim my mouth with his.

5

I HAD to give it to the guy, he was a quick learner. And energetic. Before the fourth, or was it fifth, round, I almost begged him to stop so I could sleep. Somehow, he got me going again anyway. I finally fell asleep a couple of hours before dawn.

I woke to the late summer Sydney sun pouring through the window. I was tired and my body ached gloriously. Cooper was still asleep, his mouth open slightly.

"Morning." Jake stuck his head through the door. He looked rested. He must have slept with earplugs in and his smart watch on vibrate in case he was needed. "I've ordered breakfast from Scarlett's. It should be here soon."

I stretched, too sleepy to do more than mentally

acknowledge that the covers were down to my stomach. It was nothing Jake hadn't seen before. "You're the best."

Money could buy a lot of things, but it couldn't buy the ability to cook. Neither of us had bothered to learn beyond making coffee and toast. When you own several restaurants, and have a private chef on call, it's a skill you don't need.

"Yeah, I know," he said distractedly. His eyes were on my breasts. And on the guy sleeping beside me. "Did you have a good night?"

I couldn't contain a smile. "I've had worse."

Cooper stirred. He opened his eyes and seemed confused for a moment, until he remembered where he was. "Hey." He sat up and ran a hand over his head. "Last night was amazing." He looked like he couldn't quite believe it happened.

"It sounded like it." Jake pushed the door open and stepped inside. So much for wearing earplugs.

He held a handful of papers and a pen toward Cooper. "I have a bunch of shit for you to fill out. Bank details, assuming you want to be paid. Tax details. And our offer for your uncle's garage. You just need to sign that and I'll lodge it with the relevant authorities."

Jake handed that to Cooper first.

Cooper signed it without even glancing at it, then handed it back to Jake.

"Huh." Jake folded the paper in two. "We should have offered less."

Cooper sat back against the pillows. "I told you, I don't care about the place."

"You should," I told him. "The property is worth over a million dollars." It must be later than I thought, if Jake already had someone assess the value of the garage.

Cooper looked surprised but unfazed. "I'm just happy to get something for it."

He really should be more careful, but I understood. Sometimes you just needed to move on with your life.

Says the woman who bought, and lives in, the home where her parents were murdered. In spite of the memory of coming home from school as an eight-year-old to find their blood splattered all over the walls, I had a connection to the place. That and I had to keep it out of the hands of the Onyx Ridge pack. It was the principle of the thing. Of course, I had the whole place gutted and completely remodelled before I moved in. Clinging to memories is one thing. Living inside my own personal PTSD is another.

"You can fill out the rest of the forms later," I said. "I'm going to have a shower, then we can work out what your role in the organisation will be."

Okay, I admit it, I pushed the covers off myself and walked naked to the bathroom in part to punish Jake for being all business this early in the morning. Especially after the night I had. I knew he did it to remind me not to get caught up in Cooper's pretty face and smoking hot body. I didn't need the reminder. Hadn't I proven to him yet that I knew how to put business before pleasure? If I didn't, I would have fucked his face a thousand times and not regretted any of them.

Both sets of eyes followed me until I closed the door. I listened for a moment, but it didn't sound like they were going to kill each other, so I stepped into the shower and washed myself of dried sweat and cum.

By the time I was clean and dry, my hair back in a ponytail, light make-up on my face and dressed in a knee length pencil skirt and a white silk blouse, breakfast had just arrived.

The guys sat at the table near the kitchen, in front of the wide window. Judging by his damp hair, Cooper had a shower in one of the other bathrooms.

"Jake said you wouldn't mind if I had a scrub," Cooper said.

I slipped into a chair. "Did he offer to wash your back?" I snagged one of the cups of coffee and peeled back the lid. It smelled divine.

"Of course I did," Jake said. "What sort of host would I be if I didn't?" He grinned and pushed a bowl of fruit salad, oats and yoghurt towards me.

I made a face. "I was hoping for pancakes."

"I know you were," Jake said. "I'm here to make sure you don't put that shit in your body, like you asked me to."

"This from the guy who had a whole jar of sugary cherries last night." I rolled my eyes at him.

"At least they're fruit," he pointed out.

"Just barely." I sipped my coffee. At least he didn't complain about me drinking that.

Cooper looked from one of us to the other. "Are you two always like this?"

"Smoking hot and as funny as fuck?" Jake asked. "Yes. Yes we are."

I snorted. "Jake likes to think he is my father."

"No," Jake corrected. "I like to think I'm your daddy. There's a significant difference." He wiggled his brows at me.

Cooper grinned. "You guys are awesome. I

thought you might be all scary and shit, and you are," he added quickly, "but you're also really cool."

"Yeah. I am pretty cool for an old dude," Jake agreed.

"You're not that old," I told him. I tried not to think about the age difference between Cooper and Jake. There I was, just about bang in the middle. Okay, now I was thinking about being in the middle of them, the meat in a hot-guy sandwich. Sometimes it was hard to remember why I didn't sleep with Jake.

"No, I just feel like it sometimes." Jake looked towards Cooper. "Be careful. Hanging around with Ivory might cause you to age before your time. Before you know it, your teenage years will be over." He snapped his fingers.

"I turn twenty soon," Cooper said.

"It's started already." Jake grinned.

I picked up a slice of banana and threw it at him. It hit him in the side of his head, then fell into his lap.

He looked down at it. "I should insist you come over here and eat that."

Did he have any idea how much I wished I could?

He picked up the slice, threw it up in the air and

caught it in his mouth. He grinned at his own prowess.

Cooper clapped.

"Don't encourage him," I said. "Sometimes I think he should have joined the circus."

"Sometimes I'm pretty sure I *did* join the circus," Jake said.

I stuck my middle finger up at him.

He grinned, but he looked like he would happily take my finger and suck on it for a while.

"So… Can I ask what the story is between the Onyx Ridge pack and Ivory Claw?" Cooper asked tentatively.

That brought down the atmosphere.

I sighed. "Many, many years of bad blood. My parents ran the dominant pack in the city. And my father's parents before them. The Dagens gathered enough power to move against them. They slaughtered my parents and a lot of other white wolves. They took over the territory. They ran it until about seven years ago, when I took it back."

"You were young when that happened?" Cooper asked softly.

"I was eight." I looked down at the table. "They liked to think they had morals, or some shit like that, so they didn't kill the children. They just sent us off to live with various associates of the Dagen family. I was raised here in Sydney by Helen Dagen, Alastair's aunt. It was her job to brainwash me into thinking my role in life was as the omega of their pack."

I looked back up and smiled savagely. "She was one of the first people I had killed."

"Taking out that hag was a pleasure." Jake had a self-satisfied smirk on his face.

"What about you?" Cooper asked him. "What were you doing? You wouldn't have been a kid, I'm guessing."

"I was doing what any smart wolf would do," Jake replied. "What most of us were doing. Biding our time and waiting for the right chance, and the right person to fight back against Dagen. The moment I saw Ivory, I knew she was the person we were waiting for. She was so full of anger and hate. The stupidest thing Barnaby Dagen did was not kill her. He didn't see the rage inside her. He was so sure he won, he didn't even think to look."

"He was so sure we were all broken," I said. "If he won me at that auction, he might have been right. Everyone was happy to join me when I started to move against Dagen, but no one dared to start it before me."

"No one else had the guts," Jake said. "That

includes me. If Dagen knew you would grow up to be a banana throwing pancake lover, he would have been shaking in his shoes."

I laughed. "That does sound terrifying, doesn't it?"

Cooper was staring at me with open admiration. "For a long time, I've heard about you and how badass you are, but you're next level. I can't believe I got to fuck you. Anytime you want to do it again, I'm here for it."

I believed him. The truth was, he was as easy to like as he was hot. If I was honest with myself, I would admit I could fall head over heels for a guy like him. The gods knew that would complicate my life even further. Not to mention my relationship with Jake.

In spite of not wanting to cross the line, I did love him. I loved him from the moment he won my auction, when he looked at Dagen with a smug expression on his handsome face. Dagen was a vengeful bastard, but even then the financial cracks were starting to show. Given time, his empire would have probably imploded without me lifting a finger. I just helped it along a bit.

Jake bidding against Dagen in the first place showed the world he had balls after all. That the

Ivory Claw pack was not as beaten down as people thought. Stepping up could have gotten him killed. Instead, he helped me to get a whole lot of other people killed.

Jake sighed. "Welcome to my world, kid. You work for her now. The only time your cock will get near her, will be in your dreams."

"Is that what happened to you two?" Cooper asked. "Because you obviously have the hots for each other. I can smell it on both of you. Hells, it would be obvious to a human."

One of Jake's eyebrows twitched. "Do you always say the first thing that comes out of your mouth?"

"Yeah," Cooper admitted. "It gets me into trouble occasionally. But I'm not wrong."

"Sometimes it's not as simple as wanting to do something," I said softly. "You have to think about the consequences of doing it." The bad as well as the good.

"But you admit you want to fuck me?" Jake cocked his head and looked smug.

So. Fucking. Much.

I cocked my head at him. "Did I ever say I didn't?"

"Hell yeah." Jake grinned. He and Cooper shared a high-five.

Men.

I rolled my eyes at them. "Has it ever occurred to you that this, right here, is why I won't sleep with you? Because you need to grow the fuck up?"

They exchanged amused looks.

Jake shook his head. "Naw. You like my boyish enthusiasm."

He wasn't wrong. But that didn't make any of this simpler or easier.

"Sex complicates things," I said.

"I dunno, it seemed pretty simple to me," Cooper said. "I wanted you. You wanted me."

"If the next words out of your mouth are, 'wham bam, thank you ma'am,' you're fired," I said dryly.

Cooper grinned. "I don't know what that means, but I am grateful for last night. And I promise I can do whatever work you give me to do and focus on that, whether we're sleeping together or not."

"Maybe I'm the one who can't focus," I suggested.

"Ohhh, now I get it." Jake slapped a hand to his forehead. "All this time I thought you were worried I couldn't do my job. But it's you who are distracted by my devastating good looks."

I drummed my fingernails on the table. "Exactly. If you had a head like a potato, there would be no problem." I held back a laugh.

"So you would rather fuck someone that looks like a potato than fuck me?" Jake pouted.

I pretended to think about that for a moment. "They would have to have some a-peeling characteristics, but maybe."

Both guys laughed.

It felt good to sit around the table and chat like… Like friends. For a while at least, I could forget about the world, the Dagens and all that shit. We could almost be normal people. Almost.

"For the record," I said slowly, "I want to fuck both of you. I just don't want any of us to end up dead because of it. Is that so terrible?" It made sense to me.

"Sometimes life is too short to be sensible." Cooper sounded like an old man.

"That's fucking deep, kid," Jake said. He jerked his head sideways, towards Cooper. "He's right though. You spent ten years of your life living with a Dagen. You could have married one and had mutant puppies. Instead, you offered yourself up for auction and took back what was ours. You spent nearly a decade taking chances with almost everything. Everything but your heart."

"That's fucking deep, old man." Cooper smiled.

"Isn't it though?" Jake said. To me he said, "I get it.

We walked through the fire together. You think if we had a relationship outside friendship and work, and it ended, we would end."

"Wouldn't it?" I asked. "Just think, you could go on social media and complain about your psychotic ex. Isn't that what people do?"

"Have you ever seen me on social media?" Jake asked. Then softly he added, "You and I wouldn't end."

"You don't know that," I said. I noticed he didn't deny I was psychotic.

"Yes I do," he said firmly. "We are a team. Now and forever. Even if you wanted to get rid of me, you couldn't."

"I could have you killed," I pointed out. They wouldn't like it, but my men would do it if I asked them to.

"But you wouldn't," he said with certainty. "We've been through too much together to end that way." He gave me a long, intense stare.

"See?" Cooper said. "The sexual tension in here is through the roof. You two should just fuck and get it over with. But also me too. I don't mind sharing."

"The kid is wise," Jake said. "That sounds like a plan to me."

"I'm glad you two have it all worked out." I gave

them both a dark look. "Maybe I should step outside and leave you both to it." Yeah okay, when I thought about that for a second, it was hot as fuck.

"Not without you," Cooper said. "But I wouldn't say no to a threesome."

Before I could respond to that, we were interrupted by a knock on the door.

"Saved by the bell," I said under my breath. I nodded for Jake to open the door.

"Morning boss, sorry to interrupt," Kyle said. He looked anxious.

"Actually, your timing is perfect," I said. "Is there a problem?"

"I'm not sure," he admitted. "I took those artefacts to Rachel, like you asked. She just got back to me about them. Something is really screwy."

6

"Screwy in what way?" I looked down at the box that sat open on Rachel's desk. Jake stood beside me. Cooper gawked at the magic shop. Most of it was fake magic, designed to amuse humans. She kept the real stuff behind a magic wall. It all made me want to twitch. At the best of times, magic gave me the creeps. Screwy magic most of all.

Rachel brushed a strand of dark hair back over her ear. "Screwy in that most of them don't have any in them." She picked up a bright white stone that was shaped like a donut, and held it in the palm of her hand.

"This is just a rock. I sell the same kind of thing here. A witch can put a protection spell in it, or whatever." She shrugged. "Nothing very powerful."

I knew that, because I wouldn't let her sell them otherwise. Protection spells were harmless unless they protected someone I was trying to dispense with. Since they only protected against magic, they weren't much use against big teeth anyway.

"Is there any chance it had magic in it but it was used up?" Jake said.

"Almost certainly," she agreed. "There's a residue of magic in it. I can't tell what kind. The point is, like this, it's worthless. Not something the black market would bother with." She put the stone back and picked up another. "Same with this one. Except this one," she held up between her thumb and forefinger. "This is a bonding stone. Or it would be if it wasn't empty."

"Bonding stone." Jake took the stone from her hand and bounced it up and down on his palm a couple of times. "Two people touch it, and when their cum is combined, they form an… Empathic connection?" He gave me a speculative glance.

"That's what it's for," Rachel said. "Empty, it's just a rock."

"Could you fill it?" Jake asked.

"No," I said firmly. Even if I wanted to form a psychic bond with him, I would never fuck with magic like that. There was no telling what it might do to us in the long run. It might drive us insane, or turn us into assholes.

"I can't anyway," Rachel said. "I don't have that kind of magic. Very few witches do." She took back the stone and replaced it in the box.

She picked up a pair of silver tweezers and pulled out another. "This one does have magic in it. Specifically, it's a magic dampening stone. The kind used to stop witches from doing magic. That's why I won't touch it with my bare hands. The weird thing is, they're usually put into bracelets. Just by itself, a witch could just drop it if they wanted to, and the effect would be gone."

"I'm sensing a pattern here," Jake said. "Silas Wheeler might have just been selling these to a witch to be filled, or have a bracelet made."

"Or Dagen is trying to send us a message," I said. "The white stone can't be a coincidence. The rest of it…" I shook my head. "Couldn't he just send a letter, or a text, like a normal person?"

Cooper must have heard his uncle's name mentioned, because he appeared at my shoulder. "Did you send his father any cryptic messages before you went after the Onyx Ridge Pack?"

"Not unless you call dead bodies cryptic," I said.

There was nothing subtle about the slaughter we inflicted on the black wolves. We splattered their blood the way they splattered ours.

"White stone, bond, dampening," Jake mused. "What about the other three?"

"The black one shaped like a doughnut has some residual power in it," Rachel said. "It feels similar to the white one, but I still can't tell what it is. And that," she pointed, "is a siphon stone. Also empty." She shuddered.

"Used to suck out a witch's magic," Cooper said, his eyes wide.

"Even empty, that's worth more than the rest of them put together," Jake said.

"And the last two aren't magical at all," I said softly. "That's a bloodstone. And that's a black diamond." I knew my precious gems. "Black diamonds represent death. He is trying to tell us he is more powerful than we are. That he will siphon off all our work into his bank accounts and that the Onyx Ridge pack will bring about our death with lots of blood."

"What about the other two?" Cooper asked. "Bonding and dampening?"

"Nothing good," Jake said. "He knew we were

going to put Silas down. He made sure this was waiting for us. How did he know?" He looked accusingly at Cooper.

Cooper raised his hands to either side and stepped back. "I've no idea. It was nothing to do with me, I swear. Silas probably didn't know either. He was just a go-between."

"Between Dagen and who?" Jake asked. "If we hadn't grabbed these, who would have?"

"It was always going to be us," I said softly. "Either he told Silas to leave them on his desk until we turned up, or one of our people is working for Dagen."

"It's not me," Cooper said. "I never even saw the box until today."

"For the record, it's not me," Rachel said. "Break-ins in the area have been way down since you guys took over. It's saved me thousands in replacement costs and repairs. I am a big fan." She smiled at me but it held a tinge of anxiety. Like she wasn't sure if I believed her or not.

I nodded. I had no reason to think the witch was in cahoots with Dagen. Our dealings had always been beneficial to both of us, and she was paid well each time.

"We know it isn't Ivory or me," Jake said. "That only leaves a couple thousand other people as possibilities." His tone was light but his face was worried. If Dagen was behind this, it might be the start of something bigger. And probably annoying.

I rubbed my forehead with my fingertips. I didn't need him doing shit.

"They might only be stones," Cooper said. "Just because it seems like they meant something doesn't mean they do. Black diamonds are worth a lot. The rest have some use."

"Except the bloodstone," I pointed out. "That's probably worth about three dollars. Why put that in there unless it has some meaning?" I looked around, but none of them had any more answers than I did.

"I could shove it down his throat for you," Jake offered.

"Fuck," Cooper said. "I was going to say the same thing."

Jake grinned. "Rock, paper, scissors for the privilege?"

I rolled my eyes at them both. "No one is going to shove it down his throat. You wouldn't get close enough anyway. If we could, I would happily do it myself."

Both guys looked disappointed.

I glanced at Rachel and shrugged. Men, what could you do?

She grinned in response.

I tapped my fingers on my thigh. "Alistair Dagen wouldn't have handled these himself. He would have had someone do it for him. Coop, any idea who might have done that?"

He thought for a moment. "People came and went all the time. I didn't pay much attention to them when I was there. Which wasn't often."

"But you knew he was dealing with Dagen," Jake pointed out.

"Only because he told me. We argued about it." Cooper scratched his cheek. "I'm not sure if he dealt directly with them. There might have been a go-between."

"If Dagen knew we were working through Silas' garage, then he would want to keep his hands clean," I said. "He wants us to know he is involved, but doesn't want us to be able to prove it. If we make any kind of move against him, he could claim it was unprovoked."

"I'd like to know how many fucking pies he also has his fingers in," Jake said. He looked furious, like if we missed anything, he would blame himself.

"Let's find that out," I said. "Do a full check on any of the small side businesses. These are the pies he'll stick his fingers in first." After a moment I added, "And Crimson. He was there last night. The gods only knew what he might have gotten up to. Or tried to."

Jake nodded. "I'll get on it. But subtly. If he knows we're looking, he might act sooner."

"I have no doubt he will know," I said. "He sent us a warning. He wants us on edge." He certainly got that.

"Can we send him a warning back?" Cooper asked.

"We could send him your uncle's head?" Jake said lightly. "That's always a fun gift."

"Nothing says subtle like a decapitated head in a box," I said sarcastically.

"Why does it have to be subtle?" Cooper asked. "I've only seen this guy from a distance and I want to punch him in the face."

"He does have that effect on people," I agreed. "But it would have to be subtle because we can't be seen to provoke them. If Dagen wants a war, then that's what he'll get, but we won't be the ones to start it. Not officially." Unofficially, all bets were already fucking off, as far as I was concerned.

I picked up the black diamond, half expecting it to explode in my face or some shit like that. Instead, it just sparkled, reflecting the light. It wasn't worth much more than a few thousand dollars, but it certainly was pretty. "Maybe I should get this made into a ring. Or a necklace." I could wear it in front of Dagen and piss him off. That would be fun.

"I know a guy," Cooper said. "Will you let me have him make it into something for you?"

"Don't have it made into a motherfucking engagement ring," Jake growled.

Cooper looked surprised. "I wasn't even thinking that." His mouth curled up in a sly smile. "Until now."

I snorted. "We met yesterday."

"When you know, you know." Cooper grinned but I suspected it was mostly for Jake's benefit. "Fine, no engagement ring. But I have something in mind." He slipped the diamond into his pocket.

"What do we do with the rest of the stones?" Jake asked.

I looked towards Rachel. "Can you sell them for us?"

"Probably," she agreed. "I also know a guy. But—even the siphon stone?"

"Only a witch can use it on another witch, can't

they?" I asked. "If it's no threat to any wolves, then I don't care."

If witches wanted to fuck with each other, that was their business, as long as they stayed out of my way.

"Okay." If that bothered Rachel, she didn't show it. She would get a nice cut of the proceeds anyway.

"Ivory, you should put the bloodstone in your house," Jake said.

When I looked at him questioningly, he said, "Humans think they have the ability to cleanse toxins out of your body."

I gave him a flat stare. "The more you say things like that, the more I want a really big slice of cake."

Cooper chuckled.

"I'm just looking out for you," Jake said sulkily.

"I appreciate that," I assured him. "Why don't you take it, you eat more crap than I'm allowed to."

He shrugged, but slipped the stone into his pocket. It would probably turn up somewhere at my place or at Crimson sooner or later.

Rachel closed the box and took it over to a safe in the corner.

"We are all going to have to watch ourselves," I said quietly. "Watch our backs. It might start with something small like this, but at some point he's going to come after us. It could get ugly." I should probably keep Cooper away from me until all of this blew over. It *would* blow over, I was certain of that. There was no way I was going to let Dagen win. By the time this was done, he'd wish he hadn't even looked my way. He should have dug himself a hole and crawled inside. The way they tried to make me do.

"I just remembered something," Cooper said.

His tone immediately had my attention, and my concern.

"What is it?" I asked. And why did I suddenly have a sense of dread in the pit of my stomach?

"Remember when I said I told my uncle to ask you for help?" When I waved at him to continue, Cooper said, "According to him, he had it under control."

"He was lying," Jake said simply.

Cooper shook his head. "You knew him. He was a terrible liar. He couldn't lie his way out of Swiss cheese."

"He's right," I said. "That was why we were working with him to start with. He was an unscrupulous little worm, but we always knew when he was full of shit."

"That was most of the time," Jake said.

"Exactly." I nodded. "He was never able to hide anything from us. Not for long anyway. So when he said he thought he was in control, he must have meant it. Or thought he did."

"How the fuck though?" Jake asked. "Was he high at the time or—"

"I don't think so," Cooper said, his brow furrowed in thought. "Not that time anyway. He just seemed really sure he was all over it."

"He must've had help from someone." I tapped my fingers on my thigh.

"Dagen?" Jake asked.

"No," Cooper said after a moment. "He was more scared of… I mean just as scared of him as he was of you."

I raised my eyebrows at the suggestion that Dagen could be scarier than me. Rude.

"Someone else then," Jake said. "Who? Did he mention someone?"

Cooper scrunched up his face in the most adorable way, obviously thinking furiously. "I feel like he mentioned someone, but the name won't come to mind."

"Was he trying to sell the garage?" Jake asked. "That would have solved all his problems. Well, all his financial problems. It wouldn't change the fact he fucked up so badly with us."

Cooper shook his head. "I don't think so. My uncle wasn't the smartest wrench in the toolbox, but he was proud. I think he was hoping if he kept paddling, the tide would turn his way at some point. There was never a chance of that though, was there? Not while Dagen was trying to use him to get to you. I mean, us."

"Not unless there was a mystery person helping him," I said. "Can you find out who it is? Your uncle might've kept something at his house. A phone number, anything?"

"I can try," Cooper agreed. He wandered off to play around with Rachel's plastic wands.

"What are you thinking?" Jake asked.

"I'm wondering if there is someone else out there," I said slowly. "Someone who is working with or against Dagen. With or against us. The last thing we need is a war on two fronts."

He searched my face carefully. "You're thinking Silas was working with Zeta, or the Witch's Council, or someone like that?"

The Witch's Council was barely a blip on my radar, but Zeta was a huge, powerful organisation with connections to several major world governments. They mostly stayed out of my way because I paid the right people, but if they wanted to cause trouble for me, they certainly had the resources to cause a lot of it.

"I hope not," I said. "I have no doubt I can take down Zeta if I have to, but it would be a lot of work and headache."

Jake raised his eyebrows at me.

Yeah, okay, it was a hells of a claim to make, and frankly one I hoped I never had to back up. It would probably cost me more than I wanted to pay to do it. Especially in stress.

"There is another possibility," I said, partly to change the subject. "The grey wolves have been neutral for a long time. If anyone was going to help Silas from getting stuck between us and the Dagens, it would be them."

"They usually stay out of shit like that," Jake pointed out. "Unless they've decided to take sides."

"I'm fine with that, as long as they take ours." I watched fondly as Cooper swished a plastic wand around in the air like he was in a movie.

"And if they don't?" Jake asked.

I sighed. "Then we're going to have to have a long conversation with their Alphas. They'll think twice about fucking with us." As long as it was only speculation, and not the start of a whole another shit fight. I didn't want to take on the black wolves while the grey wolves were nipping at my tail.

"You want me to talk to them?" Jake asked.

I tapped my hand on my thigh. "That might be a good idea, yes. Let's nip that in the bud before it bears fruit. You have a blank cheque to deal with whatever comes up." That didn't always mean money. It meant I trusted him to do whatever he had to do, offer whatever he had to offer, threaten whatever he had to threaten, to get the grey wolves to stay out of our way.

"Blank cheques are my favourite," he said. "Don't worry, by the time I'm done, they'll slink back into the shadows."

"I hope so," I said. "I need to get back to Crimson. I have a meeting with someone."

Jake frowned. "Anything I need to worry about?"

"I'm not sure," I admitted. "I'll fill you in afterward."

He hated it when I wasn't forthcoming with information, but he knew better than to ask. He would know when I was ready to tell him.

"All right, boss, I look forward to it. Come on kid, time to go. Stop playing with your wand." Jake grinned.

Cooper laughed, put down the wand and trotted back over to us like a puppy. "You're just jealous because my wand is bigger than yours."

I shook my head and followed them out while they bantered about cock size.

Men.

At least they sounded relaxed. Me, I was on edge.

THE MAN who sat across from me was attractive in a rugged sort of way. His brown hair was cut close to his scalp. The hair on his square chin was longer, but neatly trimmed. Brown eyes, almost the same colour as mine, watched me with cautious interest. He rubbed a scar which spanned the bridge of his nose, between his thumb and forefinger.

"This is an interesting place to meet." His voice was deep, almost raspy.

I sat back and toyed with the glass of apple juice in my hand. "Most people seem to like it." He requested the meeting. I chose the third floor of Crimson, because people were either uncomfortable or distracted here.

I sipped my juice and looked away from a nearby

couch, where one man was trying to inhale the cock of another. Both seemed to be thoroughly enjoying themselves. Good, that was what the place was for.

He shrugged. "I'm more a doer than a watcher. I mean, if you're interested, I'm all for it." His voice was deep, husky.

I ignored his suggestion and the way my pulse raced a little faster. "You wanted to meet me. What do you want?"

"You know who I am?" he asked. He leaned forward to pour himself a glass of juice from the jug on the table.

"I know *what* you are," I replied. That should have been enough for me to say no to him stepping foot in Crimson. My curiosity got the better of me.

"And yet, you still agreed to see me. I'm surprised your alpha allowed it." He toasted me with his glass, then took a gulp.

He was so obviously after a reaction, I didn't give him one, except to say, "The Alpha doesn't get to decide who I meet with. What's your name?"

"You can call me Hutton," he replied.

"Hutton what?" I asked.

"Just Hutton," he said simply.

"If you can't even give me that much…" I started to stand.

He exhaled in frustration. "Wait, *please*. Aaron. Aaron Hutton."

I sat back down. "Your parents were—"

"Felicity and Ray Hutton. They were murdered by Dagen, just like yours." In a moment his face turned from congenial to pent-up rage and back again.

"And yet, you decided to work for Dagen," I said coldly. I had no sympathy for people like him. He wasn't the only white wolf to make that choice. I didn't understand it. I wasn't sure I wanted to.

"I was twelve years old when that asshole murdered my parents." Hutton's tone matched my own. "Me and a couple of other boys were sent to live with Gus Dagen. You've heard of him?"

"Of course I have." I barely contained a shudder. "The Butcher of Onyx Ridge. Even among wolves, he was known for his cruelty. My people fought over who was going to put him down." I don't know who actually did it, or how, except that he got what was coming to him. Or so Jake said. I had no reason not to believe him.

"Yeah. Well, he liked to practice," Hutton said bitterly. "But his favourite thing was watching us practice on each other. Once you get in a certain level over your head, it's hard as fuck to get out again. He had us all convinced we had no choice. When the Uprising took place, I took the hint and got the fuck out of there. Went underground. I figured if Dagen saw me, I was dead. And if anyone from Ivory Claw saw me, I was just as dead. Once labelled a traitor, always a traitor." He shrugged.

"The Uprising?" I asked. "I like that. And you're right, you would have been dead. Everyone back then was very... Pissed off. They tore apart one white wolf who worked for Dagen. I don't think I would have been able to stop them from tearing apart another." Would I have tried? That was a question for back then. There was a whole other set of questions for the present.

"Why now?" I asked. "Any time in the last nine years, you could have stepped forward. But you chose today. Why?"

"I asked myself the same question. Part of me is thinking I should have just stayed hidden. But..." He rubbed the scar on his nose again. "I've heard rumblings. Dagen is trying to get support. Think whatever you want about me and stuff I did in the past, but I'm fucked if I'm gonna sit by and let the black wolves take control again. They won't make the same mistake. They won't let the children live. If they come after the Ivory Claw pack, they'll kill us all this time."

His fingers were white around his glass. I was surprised it didn't shatter in his hand.

"What are you proposing to do about it?" I asked. Clearly he was done with hiding from the world. I could relate to that. There was only a certain amount of time a person could sit by and do nothing before it drove them crazy.

"I want to join you," he said. "Whatever needs to be done, I'll do it. I have a shit load to atone for, and I know it ain't gonna be easy. My people are gonna hate me, but no more than I hate myself."

Just when I thought I couldn't hate the Dagen family more, I did. Hutton was only a few years older than me, but he'd suffered worse than I had. I was treated like a piece of rubbish, but I was never made to kill my own kind. He was right about one thing, it *wouldn't* be easy. The question was, did I need that kind of division in my organisation right now?

If Jake knew I was meeting with Hutton, he would be pissed. That was too bad, I didn't answer to him. Still, some things went beyond little white lies. Meeting a guy like Hutton was one of them, especially somewhere as public as this. I was in no illusion Jake wouldn't know by the end of the day. I would tell him if someone else didn't.

"I'll think about it," I said. "What will you do if the answer is no?"

He gave me a measured look. "You want to know if I'll go back and work for Dagen?"

"Will you?" He might decide Dagen would be the winner of this battle. This war. Only an idiot sided with the loser.

"Fuck that." His blunt response made me smile. "I won't rest until every last Dagen is in some part of the seven hells, even if I have to go there with them."

"So you're reckless?" I asked. "Reckless will get you killed. It also gets other people killed." I got where I was by being ruthless, not stupid.

He put his glass down on the table. "No, I'm not reckless. I am twenty years of anger looking for a direction to go. I haven't had that. Until now. With or without you, I will bring Dagen down. I just thought you might want in on it." He gave me a knowing smile, like he suspected I wouldn't turn down a challenge.

I hadn't yet.

I smiled back. "That's cute that you think I need an invitation. Or that I couldn't stop you with a flick of my wrist.

"Why stop me?" he asked. "I want what you want."

I regarded him for a moment. "You want death and destruction at any cost. If you start killing anyone in the Dagen pack, people are going to point the finger back at me, whether we are involved or not. They'll retaliate against me if they can't find you."

"You don't seem like the kind of woman who is scared of a little retaliation. Or much of anything else." His eyes lingered on my chest for a moment before he looked back in my eyes.

"I'm not," I replied coolly. "I also don't want to give Dagen the excuse to attack us."

"It's cute that you think he needs an excuse," Hutton said. The guy was getting more cocky by the moment.

"Did he send you?" I asked.

Hutton's face turned a fascinating shade of pink. He rubbed hard at his scar with the tip of his finger.

"No. He fucking did not. If I was anywhere near Alastair Dagen, one of us would be dead. Or both. Is that what you want? Do I have to bring his head to you on a silver platter to prove whose side I'm on?"

That sounded pretty fucking perfect to me. As if to punctuate Hutton's question, the woman on the couch near us came loudly. I turned my head to watch. She straddled one guy, while another was frantically thrusting at her rear hole.

"I think she likes the idea," I remarked.

"She certainly likes something," he agreed. "Those are some life goals right there." He gave me a look that was half suggestive, but laced with the tension of our conversation. He was clearly the kind of guy who took shit seriously, even when he wanted to joke around or flirt.

"For her, or for you?" I cocked my head at him and raised an eyebrow.

"Both," he agreed. "For one thing, she has two friends. I only have one." His eyes lingered on me.

I sipped my water. "We're friends now?"

"Friends. Allies. Whatever you want to call it. Hells, I'll even settle for fuck buddies."

I wasn't sure if the obvious erection in front of his pants was because of me, or where we were. Maybe both. This part of Crimson had that effect on people. That was one of the reasons I liked it so much. If you could stay cool and focused in a room full of people fucking, then there was hope for you.

"You know how to flatter a girl, don't you?" I said dryly.

"Honestly," he said, "I don't have a fucking clue. Dagen women are toxic. Ivory Claw women don't want to know me. I would freak the shit out of human women. Witches scare the shit out of me. Demons too."

"That doesn't leave much," I remarked.

"Yeah." He shrugged. "That's the consequences of doing bad shit, I suppose. It's lonely at the bottom." He hesitated for a moment before he added, "It's probably not that different for you. I bet you scare the crap out of every man you meet."

"Are you scared?" I asked.

"Hells yeah," he admitted. "Of course I am. Everyone here looks like they're having a good time, but I know I could be dead before I took two steps if you wanted."

"I'm sure you could make it at least *three* steps," I said.

"I'll aim for four if I have to," he said. "Even a guy like me has to have ambition."

I snorted. "You seem to have lots of that. You really think you could bring me the head of Alistair Dagen on a platter?"

"Not without help," he admitted. "That's why I'm here."

"You said you heard rumblings," I said slowly. "What did you hear and where did you hear it from?" Just like with Cooper, I wouldn't rule out the idea that Dagen sent him. Just because Helen Dagen's brainwashing didn't work on me didn't mean Gus Dagen hadn't done a number on Hutton. He obviously had, since Hutton allied himself with them, at least for a time.

"One of the guys who were sent to the Butcher with me, he's still on the inside," Hutton admitted. "He's pretty fucked up. I've been trying to get him out for the longest time. They broke him. Close enough anyway. I kept a line open between us. He didn't say much, just that something was up. He thought Dagen was planning some shit. He got scared and didn't tell me anything else. He could get eviscerated for just that much if they find out."

I would have liked a lot more information, but I suspected that was all I was going to get. He couldn't tell me what he didn't know.

"You said you'd do anything," I said. "If I asked you to go back to Dagen, would you?"

I wasn't prepared for the look of absolute dread on his face. I knew that exact feeling. It took me back to when I saw Barnaby Dagen walk through the door before the virgin auction. I was in the darkness, offstage, but I saw his strut, the determined set of his jaw. Even from a distance I felt his cold fury. He had a plan for me, but I derailed it by taking part.

I wouldn't marry the person of his choice and be a dutiful little beaten down omega. I defied him and he would take it out on every centimetre of my body.

The memory made my stomach turn.

"No more than you would, I'm guessing," he said softly.

I shook my head to clear it. "The past doesn't matter. The only thing that does is what we do today."

"Keep telling yourself that," he said. "Someday you might even believe it. But you know as well as I do, that the past is what shapes us. It's why people hate me, and why they're scared of you. The past is everything."

"Only if we let it be," I said firmly. He was right though. My life up until this point shaped every part of me. Whether I put it aside or not, it was still there in the back of my mind.

He sat back. "Some of us don't have a choice. And the answer is no. If I go anywhere near Dagen, it will only be to kill him. That doesn't mean I still can't be useful."

I was starting to realise that rubbing his scar was something he did when he was nervous or anxious. The skin on that part of his nose must be very smooth by now. Part of me wanted to find out. It was hard not to be drawn to someone who had the same broken, fucked up start in life. Jake had kept himself out of it. Cooper was too young to have lived any of it. Ben's childhood was a different kind of fucked up. Hutton and I would bear the scars of it forever.

"What can you do?" I asked. The two men who were pounding into the woman near us were getting louder and louder. One or both of them would come soon. The sight and sound of them was arousing, I have to admit. Not for the first time, I was glad I was a woman and didn't have a hard cock to show the world.

"You must have some skills."

"I'm good with my tongue," Hutton said. Apparently I wasn't as good at keeping my thoughts to myself as I thought I was.

I rolled my eyes. "Skills we can use against Dagen."

"Right." He gave me a rueful smile."I can fight. With guns and knives, hand-to-hand. With my teeth. With my claws. I'm proficient in a couple of different martial arts. And I can bake cupcakes."

"Cupcakes?" I echoed. "You should have led with that." Jake was really *not* going to like this guy. "Can you send Dagen a dozen chocolate ones?" Shame he wouldn't be dumb enough to eat them. A girl could dream, right?

"With laxatives in them," Hutton said wistfully.

"Or better yet, fast acting poison. Is there anything undetectable that he might eat?" I wasn't quite ready to let go of this idea yet.

"I don't think we'd get close enough to give him any." Hutton sighed.

I decided against telling him Alistair Dagen was in this very building the previous night. Although, if he got sick or died from anything he ate while at Crimson, it wouldn't be hard to trace the trail back to us.

"So I'm in?" Hutton asked.

"Because you have skills with baked goods?" I asked. "It's going to take more than that."

"You have to check with your alpha first?" Hutton asked. He raised an eyebrow at me in challenge.

"Word of advice," I said coolly, "stop suggesting I answer to anyone, even as a joke. That shit got old a long time ago. I don't just give a job to anyone who walks in off the street." Or ones I bid on. "If I did, I would be overstaffed."

He leaned in towards me. "The difference between me and them is that you *need* me. If you want to stop Dagen from doing whatever he plans, I can help. I *will* help."

"Whether I like it or not?" I asked. My tone was bordering on dangerous, but his proximity and the threesome in the corner of my eye was distracting and heady.

He locked his gaze on mine and his breath brushed over my cheek. "You would definitely like it."

Shit, he must be catching the same vibe. I don't know how I had any lust left after the marathon session with Cooper, but apparently I did. I reminded myself of who he was and what people like him did. He killed members of our pack for our enemy. However muddy the reasons for doing that, it still happened.

"You think so, do you?" I said.

He licked his lips. "Without a doubt. I—"

"What the fuck?"

The first sign I had that Jake was here was the man himself charging toward us. His face looked like thunder.

"What the *shit* is he doing here?" Jake snarled.

8

Hutton jerked away. "I—"

Jake looked like he was about to shift and rip Hutton's throat out. Instead, he leaped towards him. His momentum knocked the table in front of me. Two glasses and the jug went flying.

Before I could move, I found myself covered in a couple of litres of ice cold apple juice.

The front of my white silk blouse was absolutely saturated. Juice dripped from my face, from my arms, from my hair.

Jake froze, his hands out to either side. "Oh. Shit." He stepped towards me. "Ivory… I'm so sorry."

I could only manage one word. *"Fuck."*

He reached for me to—I don't even know what. He was useful, but he wasn't a motherfucking towel.

I sidestepped him. "What the hells?" I growled under my breath.

"He's a traitor," Jake said. He turned to Hutton. "Get the fuck out." He waved towards the door.

Hutton took a step away.

"He's here at my request," I said coldly. "We are not done talking yet. I need to get clean. Don't kill each other."

"I make no guarantees," Jake said. "You can wait for us in the ground floor bar, asshole. I don't trust you running around up here. Before you have any thoughts, security is everywhere." He waved Ben over from the door and gestured for him to escort Hutton out.

Hutton shrugged. "I have no plans to try anything."

"You better fucking not," Jake snarled. "I should kill you myself and get it over with, but that would ruin the mood in here. Ivory hates it when people do that." He was angry, but he obviously hadn't missed the fact the juice made my blouse practically transparent. His erection pressed at the front of his pants.

I glared at him, then stomped past him towards the elevator. Men and their stupid need to out-dick each other. Did he really think I didn't know what I was doing?

Maybe I should kill them both and get it over with.

I stepped into the elevator and pressed the button to close the door before Jake could get inside. Recognising that might be childish and he might change his mind and actually kill Hutton, I pressed the other button to open the door again. I crossed my arms over my chest and stepped back to let Jake join me in the elevator car.

Neither of us said a word all the way up. Or when we stepped into the apartment. Not even when I saw Cooper sitting on the couch, a book in his hand.

"Jake can explain," I said before he could ask. "Maybe you can wash my back." I slipped into the bathroom before anyone could say another word.

I shed my clothes and stepped into the shower. Closing my eyes, I leaned forward into the hot, steamy water to rinse the sticky juice off my face.

The shower door opened and closed. Strong hands gently massaged my shoulders.

I dropped my head and savoured the feeling. "Mmmm, that feels good."

"Yes, you do."

My head snapped back up. Heart thundering, I turned around and blinked water out of my eyes.

"Jake..."

He was naked, muscles slick with water, cock already hard.

I couldn't deny how freaking hot he was. "You shouldn't be in—"

His blue eyes were even more intense than usual, dark with desire. "I'm done with excuses." He gripped my upper arms, pressed me against the side of the shower and slammed his mouth against mine.

I kissed him back at first, hungrily, but forced myself to break away. It took me a moment to catch my breath. "We agreed—"

"*You* agreed," he corrected. "I never agreed that we shouldn't touch each other. I never wanted to keep my distance. I *never* agreed to be platonic." He rubbed his thumbs over my wet, bare skin, tracing circles lightly. "I've waited long enough. I'm not waiting any more." He pressed his body to mine and kissed me again.

"I want you. I know you want me." He kissed down my cheek, down my neck.

My defences were gradually evaporating, washed down the plughole. "Shouldn't you be keeping an eye on our guest downstairs?"

He paused for a moment. "Ben can handle it." He

went back to kissing my neck while his hands wandered down my sides.

"Jake…" My voice wavered.

"Please don't tell me to stop." His voice was muffled by my throat. "I'm not sure I can."

I knew there was no way in hells he would ever force himself on me. He knew I knew that. He might make me sticky, but he'd never hurt me.

I placed my fingers on his chest and pushed him back hard enough to dislodge his mouth. "If this changes everything…"

He placed his hands on either side of my face. "It won't. I promise. We're just giving each other what we know we want and need." Water poured down on us both. His eyes bore into mine, searching like he was looking for my soul.

I wasn't sure he would find one.

I swallowed hard. The last piece of resistance crumbled like a sand castle at high tide. *Gods, please let this be the only thing that falls apart.* If I lost him because of this, I would never forgive myself.

"Please… *don't* stop," I said softly.

His mouth crashed into mine. His tongue pushed its way between my lips, demanding entry, tasting my teeth, my tongue. Without words, he was telling me to let go. Let him be in control.

I melted against him.

He kissed his way down my cheek, down my chest. When he reached my nipples, he licked and sucked them mercilessly. Until all I could do was pant from the pleasure he sent smashing into my core.

Just when I thought I might go wild from that, he dropped to his knees. He firmly pushed my legs apart and dove in, face first. His tongue massaged my clit, licked over my folds like he was starving for a meal.

I pressed my palms against the tiles behind me to keep myself upright, and dropped my head back. Water gushed down over me. Body jets teased my nipples. I had them placed at exactly that height for a reason. Another one was positioned right behind where Jake's head currently was. Why not have fun in the shower?

My breath came in ragged pants.

Gods, I had imagined this for so long. Too long. I remembered my words to Hutton, about letting the past define us. I had done exactly that. And let fear guide me. Ironic that I could take on a pack of black wolves, but I was scared of a man who loved me, whom I loved in return.

"Jake," I moaned softly. "I'm going to come." I

teetered right on the edge of the precipice, but my orgasm was still building like a dam trying to breach its walls.

He drew his face back and smiled up at me. "Not yet you're not. Not till I say so. I am the alpha here."

At any other time, that would have pissed me off. Here, it turned me on.

I laughed from deep in the back of my throat. "Do I call you daddy?" I teased.

He chuckled. "Beautiful El, you can call me whatever you like. Just say it loud. And not until I say so."

"Asshole," I grumbled playfully.

"That's me." He went back to eating my pussy.

I watched him while he did it. My eyes drank in his muscular body, deliciously covered in ink. That much of it wouldn't suit some guys, but it looked perfect on him. Sexy as fuck. My own skin, in contrast, was as pale as my hair. Flawless apart from a freckle here and there. The tattoo on my back and a small one on my wrist were all I wanted.

One of his hands gripped my thigh, the other crept around to grab my ass. Between them both, he held me firmly.

I inched closer and closer. The rebellious part of me wanted to come, whether he said I could or not. I wouldn't be me if I didn't at least think it.

The rest of me wanted, needed, to do what he said, to let him take control.

"I'm close," I said. I lightly rolled my hips, seeking more and more.

He pulled his face away. "Not yet."

Without his touch I drew back from the edge. I groaned. "Please. I need to come."

He grinned and wiped water off his face with one hand. "I think I like it when you beg. I might have to get you to do it more often."

I snorted. "Don't push it, buddy."

He chuckled and pressed his face back between my legs.

I moaned. *"Please."*

He rubbed his hand over my ass, and dipped it down between my legs. The tip of his finger grazed over my rear hole.

My knees quivered.

Encouraged, he pressed the tip of his finger inside me, while his tongue teased the entrance to my pussy.

"Mmmm," I groaned. "That feels so good."

He pressed his finger in further and thrust it in and out in rhythm with his tongue.

"Oh gods." I closed my eyes and savoured the sensations coursing through my body, making my pulse spike. "I can't not… I have to…"

"Not yet." His words were muffled but firm.

I growled, deep in the back of my throat.

He chuckled and pulled his face away long enough to say, "I can stop."

"Don't you dare." I glared at him with narrowed eyes but a smile tugging at the corners of my mouth. "Fucking clit tease."

He wiggled his eyebrows and went on doing what he was doing so well. He drove me closer to the edge and held me there, drew me back, then drove me forward again.

"I think you've been obedient long enough," he said between licks and flicks of his thumb over my clit. "Come for me."

Almost immediately, I came, panting and moaning as warm water and hot pleasure washed down over my body. I was lost in a whirlpool, a torrent, a flood that carried me away until every nerve ending in every part of me was singing.

Just as I hit the peak of my orgasm, Jake rose, turned me around and bent me over so the palms of my hands were pressed against the tiled seat to the side of the shower.

"Keep your hands there," he ordered. He gripped my hips and slid his cock deep into my pussy.

Instead of coming down, I came again at the feeling of him inside me. Harder and faster the second time, until I couldn't remember my name or where I was. I didn't care. I was lost in the most delicious place. I never wanted to leave.

Jake muttered something like, "Should have been more assertive sooner," and started to thrust slowly.

Maybe he should have, but I might have pushed him away anyway. Recent events made me realise life was too fucking short to deny stuff you shouldn't. That didn't matter now. What mattered was right here, in the present.

"You feel incredible," he whispered. "I had forgotten just how incredible. It's been too fucking long." He punctuated each word with a thrust.

All I could do in response was to say, "Mmmm," and wriggle my ass a little.

He smacked my ass cheek. "Sassy little minx."

"I'm not a cat," I retorted.

"No, but you have one hells of a pussy," he said.

I should have seen that one coming a kilometre away.

I closed my eyes and rocked my hips back and forth in rhythm with him. "And you're not a rooster."

He chuckled. "Just think how long you've been missing out on one hells of a cock."

I could have reminded him that I hadn't been short on cock over the last nine years, but that didn't seem like the classy thing to do. Instead, I said, "Anything worth having is worth waiting for." He knew the truth of that.

"Yes, you are," he agreed. "One million percent worth it."

For the longest time he kept a slow, leisurely pace, while I supported my way to the front of my hands and enjoyed the feeling of being with him. I try to remember why I denied us both this, but right now I couldn't. It all made sense at the time, if not now.

Gradually, his thrusts got faster. He slid his hands up my stomach and cupped my breasts. He palmed my already hard nipples.

"El, you drive me fucking wild, woman," he said breathlessly. "Absolutely feral."

"Just the way I like you," I said. "Wild and vicious."

He pinched my nipples hard enough to make me gasp in surprise. "Vicious like that?"

"Mmmm, yeah, like that." He wasn't the first partner to get rough, but it was the first time he got rough with me. I liked it.

He slapped my ass harder this time. Then again and again until it stung.

"Who is the boss?" he asked. "When I fuck you, who is in charge?"

"I am the boss," I replied, "except when you fuck me." Then it was up for debate, but I was happy to let him lead this time. Wait. This time? Was I really ready to accept that the line between us was gone now? That was a question for later.

"I won't forget it if you don't." He slapped my ass again, then gripped my hips. "I'm going to come inside you."

My whole body quivered. "Yes, please." Each thrust drove me closer to coming again.

"Say that again, louder," he insisted. "Tell me what you want me to do."

I turned my head to look over my shoulder. "I want you to come inside me, please. *Please*." On the last word, I came again and so did he.

The whole world disappeared in a haze of frantic thrusting, panting, heat and pleasure.

I was pretty sure I screamed his name loud enough for all of Sydney to hear. I didn't care. Let them hear. Let them know I finally gave in to my long standing desire to fuck Jake. He deserved to hear it after being patient for so long. I deserved it too, because keeping him at arm's length was the right thing to do.

He grunted my name over and over. "El, Elodie, Elodie..." Then he slumped forward, his hands still gripping my hips.

Slowly and reluctantly, he slid out of me and helped me to straighten back up. His eyes searched mine. I knew he didn't want to ask, but he needed to know the answer.

"Any regrets?"

I could have said I did and shattered his heart into a thousand pieces. Instead, I decided to be honest.

I shook my head, my wet hair swinging and spraying droplets this way and that. "None. I know you think it's unfair that I pushed you away for so long—"

He pressed two wet fingers against my lips. "I understand why you did it. It was the right thing. At the time. We had to focus on..." He waved a hand around us. "All of this. Not just for us, but for the generations who will carry on the pack after us."

"That is legitimately the wisest fucking thing anyone has ever said in this shower." I smiled. "Probably in any shower, anywhere, ever."

He chuckled. "I can be wise when I want to." His expression turned serious again. "Can you promise me something?"

"That depends what it is," I said. I didn't want to make any promises I couldn't keep.

He looked me directly in the eyes and said, "Can you promise not to push me away again? I don't want this to be a one time thing. I want to be with you. Even if that means sharing you with guys like Cooper and Ben. I mean, at this point I think we would have to chase Cooper away with a stick, or have him killed. And he's, you know, a nice kid. But you and I, we've taken a step forward. I don't want to take a step back again." He cocked his head at me and gave me his best puppy dog eyes.

"I—" I considered how to respond. "I don't want to push you away again. But if I feel like it's putting either of us into the shit, I will have no choice. If we can still work together and not fuck this up, then… We can see how it goes." That was all I could give him right now.

He nodded slowly. "Fair enough. I know we can do this. I know I can. You're the most incredible fucking woman I've ever met. The second I laid eyes on you, I knew I would never get over you. If Dagen won that auction, I would have had no choice but to tear him to pieces to keep him from touching you."

"And that's the most romantic thing anyone has ever said in this shower," I said. What can I say? I'm a sucker for guys who want to spread the blood of my enemies across the nearest wall. I would do the same for them too. Strange how I already added Cooper to that. Had we only met the night before? It was hard not to be protective of him, as well as attracted to and turned on by him. The guy was both hot and adorable. Like Jake.

"I will try to remember to make daily, romantic death threats against people for you," Jake said with a smile. "Especially if doing that turns you on."

"It really does," I agreed.

He sighed and his smile faded. "I guess we better deal with the asshole downstairs."

I put a hand on his arm. "Not without me. Do you have any idea what he's been through?"

Jake shook his head. "No, but I know what he did. Him and guys like him. They used to tail Dagen Senior like pack of fucking puppies."

"That's why you recognised him on sight?" I asked.

"Yeah." He placed his hands lightly on either side of my face. "I don't want a guy like that anywhere near you."

"I can take care of myself," I said.

"I know you can, but guys like him are trouble. I saw the way he was looking at you. If you give him an in, he'll take it. Worst case scenario, he'll betray you to Dagen. Best case scenario I'll end up sharing you with him."

"Is that what this is about?" I asked, only half teasing.

Jake kissed my mouth hard in response."I will always have a part of you no other guy will. You could have twenty lovers and no one could ever take that away from us."

"Twenty?" I mused. "That sounds like a lot to juggle, but I guess I could—"

"Not literally," he growled playfully. He leaned in to nip my ear.

"I don't think I could deal with that much testosterone," I said. "You can be there when I talk to Hutton, but you will back the fuck off until I decide what to do with him."

"Yes, boss," Jake replied reluctantly. "But after we're done there, I'm taking you to bed and I'm going to fuck you all night long."

9

———

"Stay close," I said to Cooper. I was clean and dry and dressed, but on edge.

"I'm happy to," Cooper said.

Jake looked surprised. It was usually him telling bodyguards to stay close to me. The fact I did it let him know how off-balance I felt. Or maybe that I actually listened to his warnings about Hutton.

"I could get Kyle and—" Jake started.

"No need," I said quickly. "Three of us will be enough to keep me safe." I hoped.

"Thank you for trusting me," Cooper said. "I was right, wasn't I?"

Jake gave him a funny look. "About what?"

"That you too needed to fuck it out," Cooper said.

"You did, didn't you? I mean, unless Ivory was alone and..."

"We did," I assured him. "Yes, you were right." I patted his chest and let my hand linger there for a moment. Not even all those orgasms could take the edge off how lickable he was.

"So..." Cooper looked awkward. He obviously had something to ask, but didn't know how to ask it. If he was going to hang around with us, he was going to have to learn to dive right in.

"So?" I arched an eyebrow at him.

"So if you and Jake are a thing..." he started tentatively.

Apparently Jake had abandoned all patience today. He said, "Ivory and I are a thing. I think she wants to be a thing with you too. That's fine with me, as long as she is happy and you don't screw with her. Or... screw with her, but don't screw her *over*."

"Oh." Cooper nodded. "That's fine with me. If that's what Ivory wants."

Did I? My romantic relationships tended to last a week or two. What was I thinking, trying to start up a relationship with not one guy but two? Especially now. I was probably thinking that life was too short and I might as well go for it.

"As long as we can all get along, let's see where this leads," I said. That was about as much commitment as I could give right now. Judging by the looks on their faces, it was enough. For now. I would worry later if they wanted me to choose between them.

In spite of telling Jake I didn't need any more security, Kyle and Layla followed us from the apartment door down to the first floor.

The moment the elevator doors slid open, I knew some shit was going down. Between the angry shouts and the stink of animosity, the mood was obviously ugly.

No prizes for guessing the reason for the mood.

At first no one noticed us entering the bar. I wrinkled my nose at the smell of stale beer and wine. Sometimes I wished I could get drunk, it looked like fun. But the smell…

"He's a traitorous motherfucker," someone shouted. "Get a rope and we'll string up the prick."

"String him up on what?" someone else asked. "Just cut his throat and be done with it."

"Naw, that'll just make a mess and get us all kicked out." At least someone kept their head.

A ripple passed through the crowd as people started to notice I was there. They moved aside like the tide parting. Some of them looked nervous now, others curious. They all knew who I was, what they didn't know was how I would react.

I stepped through the crowd to see a circle of people, all paranormal, standing around Hutton. The wolf shifter looked more resigned than scared.

Did he really think I would let him be killed here in my building? Without my order? Two people would die then, Hutton and whoever killed him. I didn't tolerate that shit on my property. Go and kill people somewhere else, don't do it here.

I glanced at Jake. He looked like he would be happy if someone had taken care of his problem before we got here. Too bad. On the other hand, it did serve to illustrate my point. If Hutton died while we were fucking, that was exactly the kind of thing I was trying to prevent by keeping Jake at arm's length.

Lucky for everyone involved that Hutton was still alive. For now.

Hutton looked very glad to see me. "I waited, like you asked," he said loud enough for everyone to hear. "Your customers aren't very hospitable."

"Not to traitorous assholes like you," a tall man growled. "Your kind aren't welcome here."

I narrowed my eyes at him. Like a typical coward, he looked away quickly.

"Let's grab a seat," I said. I waved toward a table to the side of the room.

I took a step before Hutton came running at me.

I barely had time to react, to put up my hands defensively, before he flew past me and tackled someone behind me.

I whirled around.

Hutton was wrestling on the carpeted floor with a man who held a long blade in his hand. Hutton had him pinned down but the man was fighting hard. His teeth were gritted and his eyes were on me.

"Fuck," Jake swore. "Get that knife off him. Bring up the lights. Lock the doors. See if anyone else is armed." He put an arm around me protectively and hustled me over to the bar. To a place where no one could stand behind, or jump out at us. Or at me.

My heart hammered in my chest. What the absolute fuck?

Hutton was still wrestling the would-be assassin for the knife. It was clear the man had already realised he was dead, he might as well try to finish what he came here for first. He tried to slash at Hutton's face, but only managed a slice across one cheek before Hutton grabbed his wrist and slammed it against the floor.

Cooper stepped on the attacker's arm and pressed down hard with his shoe.

The attacker snarled, but Hutton forced his hand open and snatched the knife. Before he could throw it, Ben was beside him. He took it from him and tucked the blade away on his hip.

Between the three of them, they hauled the assassin to his feet.

"How the fuck did he get that in here?" Jake growled. "Security must have been too busy watching over the traitor to do their jobs properly." He narrowed angry eyes at Ben.

Ben looked as rattled as I'd ever seen him. That is, calm except the furrowing of his brow and the lines around his eyes. If anything happened to me, he would blame himself. Jake would blame him too, even though he was supposed to watch Hutton, not the people coming and going.

I wanted to give him a reassuring smile, but I was shaken. I expected someone to come after me, but not like that. This was direct, even for Dagen. It was crude.

Blood trickled down Hutton's face from the slice

on his cheek. If it wasn't for him… A witch could heal a knife wound unless it went straight through my heart. I could have been dead right now.

"Ivory?" Jake asked softly.

His voice brought me out of myself. Here I was, the big bad wolf, the head of Ivory Claw, the… wolf mother, if you like, and I was rattled by some random asshole with a knife.

I nodded and forced my icy composure back into place. I set my gaze on the would-be assassin.

"I would ask who hired you, but it's pretty fucking obvious." My voice was pure ice. "Dagen sent you to your death."

The attacker bared his teeth. "Fuck you, bitch."

I gave him a dangerous smile. "It was going to be a quick death. Now, not so much." For calling me a bitch, I would let the guys take all the time they wanted. I inhaled the smell of fear and black wolf. The first was intoxicating. The second was nauseating.

Jake placed his hand on my lower back. "This could have been a setup." I didn't need to follow his gaze to know he looked directly at Hutton. "Convenient that he just *happened* to be there."

"I had no idea this was going to happen," Hutton argued.

"I've seen this guy before." Cooper nodded toward Hutton. "At my uncle's garage."

Hutton pressed his lips together in a firm line. "I was trying to help Silas get away from Dagen. All he had to do—"

"Save it," Jake snapped. "We don't have time for your shit right now. Take that asshole downstairs. Let's get some answers out of him." He turned to me and his expression softened. "Wanna come and join in some torture?"

I smiled. "You say the most romantic things. But I want to speak to Hutton."

"Not without me there," he insisted.

"You can come," I said. "Or you can join in the torture." I raked a fingernail slowly down the back of his hand until his breath hitched.

"You're going to make me choose between you and torturing this asshole?" His expression was pained.

I raised my eyebrows at him.

He sighed. "Fine. He probably doesn't know shit anyway." He nodded to Ben. "Get him out of here."

Ben nodded and he, Cooper and a couple of other security guys hauled the attacker away.

The crowd muttered, but most of them went

back to their drinks. The lights went back down to the normal, dim level and the doors were unlocked.

I stepped towards Hutton and looked appraisingly at his cheek. "There should be a witch around here if you want that healed." Personally, I thought it would leave an awesome scar.

He shook his head and dabbed at his cheek with his fingertips. "It's nothing."

"If you're expecting gratitude, forget it," Jake snapped.

Hutton returned his gaze unflinchingly. "I'm not expecting anything. I saw the guy and acted, that's all."

"Were you working with him?" Jake asked. He obviously wasn't going to give Hutton a millimetre.

"We can talk about this somewhere else," I said. I nodded towards the office at the back of the bar. It was for the use of the manager and senior staff at Crimson, but I liked to commandeer it from time to time.

Jake was obviously not happy, but he nodded. At least I hadn't suggested going up to my apartment. I would fight him every step of the way if I did that, and this was too public a place for an argument.

We stepped into the office and I made myself

comfortable sitting on the desk. That left the guys to stand, their eyes on each other like they were sizing each other up. Sometimes I wondered how humans didn't realise wolf shifters lived amongst them. These two had it written on every centimetre of their body, from their posture to their narrowed eyes.

Jake closed the door. "Answer the question," he demanded. "Did Dagen send you?"

"No," Hutton said firmly. "I haven't seen Alistair Dagen for nine years. I haven't been in communication with any of them. No one was happier when Barnaby and Gus Dagen were dead than I was."

"That's debatable," I said dryly. "I don't think even Alistair misses his father very much." Yeah, cry me a fucking river of blood. The bad apple didn't fall far from the tree, but I gathered there wasn't much love lost between father and son.

"No one does," Hutton said. "Killing him was a community service."

"You're welcome," Jake said. "Now, what do you want? You better give us a fucking good reason not to take you downstairs with the other asshole. I would enjoy hearing you scream."

"You usually enjoy screaming no matter who it is," I pointed out.

"Yeah, but I'd enjoy it more if it's this asshole," Jake said. "After all the things he and his friends did."

"Were fucking *made* to do," Hutton said forcefully. "You have no idea what it was like. Guys like you were sitting around, all high and mighty, ready to take credit for every move against Dagen. Meanwhile, you did absolutely fucking nothing. If anyone should be ashamed of themselves—"

Jake growled and took a step toward Hutton.

"All right," I said before this turned into a full-blown fistfight. "Those were dark days. No one came out of it unscathed."

Hutton snorted and gave Jake the side eye.

"Can I kill this motherfucker now?" Jake asked. He crossed his arms over his chest and gave Hutton a death stare.

Was it wrong that I found this whole situation really hot? The smell of testosterone, the body language, it was like a drug.

"Are you fucking kidding?" Hutton snapped. "You realise I saved her life, right?" He waved a hand towards me.

"Which I'm grateful for," I started.

"If you hadn't stepped in, someone else would have," Jake said coldly.

"Who? You?" Hutton laughed bitterly. "You were

too busy being a smug bastard to see the threat. By the time you had, it would have been too late."

"Jake doesn't have eyes in the back of his head—" I tried to say.

"I would have seen it before he touched her," Jake growled. "If not me, then one of the members of our security detail."

"Yeah, they might," Hutton said. "But you would have taken all the credit. Guys like you—"

Whatever he was about to say was interrupted by Jake driving his fist into his face. He staggered back against the wall, blood streaming onto his shirt.

"If that gets onto the carpet, I'm going to be pissed off, Jake Blakesley," I growled.

Jake shook his hand and winced. "Be pissed off at *him*. He provoked *me*."

"You're both as bad as each other," I said scathingly. I hopped off the desk, grabbed a pile of tissues out of the box and pressed them to Hutton's nose. "I'm no doctor, but that looks broken to me. Now you *are* going to need to see a witch to heal it." I dabbed gently.

"My fist is fine," Jake said. He shook it and winced.

"If you're looking for sympathy for something you did to yourself, you've come to the wrong place,"

I said over my shoulder. "I said I wanted to talk, and that's what I meant."

I lowered the tissues to get a look at Hutton's nose, and of course the blood dripped from them straight onto my blouse. I sighed. At least it wasn't more juice.

"Jake, go and get a witch to fix this," I said.

"I'm not leaving you alone with him," Jake said.

I turned around and gave him a dark look. "There is a bar full of people right outside the door. Leave it open if you have to."

"I'm not gonna hurt you," Hutton said.

"I think he's more worried you're going to fuck me," I said.

Hutton looked surprised, but then he smiled although it obviously hurt. "I mean, happy to oblige."

I held up my arm to stop Jake from lunging at him again.

He grunted in frustration. "Ivory has better taste than that anyway."

"Not if she's screwing you," Hutton said. He glanced at me. "No offence. He just seems like kind of a dickhead."

"Jake has his moments." I looked back at him and smiled fondly.

"I have lots of moments," Jake said. "I'll get that

witch. If anyone is willing to help this asshole. Don't blame me if they don't." He stalked out the door and left it open behind him.

"He's right about that," Hutton said. "They might be happy to let me suffer."

"They might," I agreed. "But I won't. They'll do as they're told. It's not as though I'm giving them a choice." As much as I hated messing with witches and magic, they had their uses once in a while. One or two of them owed me favours, which would come in useful when the time came.

"You said you were trying to help Silas Wheeler," I said.

Hutton shrugged one shoulder. "He was an old friend. From before. He was one of the guys sent to live with the Butcher. Every time anyone looked at him the wrong way, he would cry or piss his pants. Gus got tired of him and sent him away. He must have had a use for him, or he would have just had him killed. We kept in contact. He tried to get out, but Dagen is like quicksand. You get one foot out and..." He shrugged. "They grab hold of the other foot and pull you back in. I told him I was going to come to you, plead my case. I said if you would listen to me, I would put a good word in for him."

He shook his head. "Silas didn't buy it. He said he

had it sorted out. He wouldn't tell me why or how, but he said he had a plan."

I nodded slowly. "It sounds like Dagen might have cancelled his debt in return for something. The gods only know what. Or if he carried it out before he died." Either way, if he was working with Dagen, he deserved what he got even more than I thought.

Hutton nodded towards my chest. "Sorry about the blood."

I looked down and grimaced. "I'm starting to get used to it." I might have to start sending Jake the bill for the dry-cleaning. Lately, every time he was around, I got messy. Sometimes good messy. Sometimes not.

Hutton gave me a funny look, but nodded. "I meant what I said. I'm not going to hurt you."

"I'm not that easy to hurt," I said. "But thank you for stopping me from having a knife in my back. That would really have spoilt my day." Not to mention my blouse.

"I believe you," he said. "The Queenmaker seems to think you're made of glass."

I blinked at him. "Is that what they're calling him now? Queenmaker?" I laughed. "That would go straight to Jake's head."

"He doesn't need an ego boost," Hutton said dryly.

"True that," I said. There was nothing wrong with having a healthy ego. I looked up at Hutton and wondered what the hells I was going to do with him, and how I could stop him and Jake from killing each other.

Jake hurried back into the office. "The witch is going to have to wait. We have a bigger problem."

10

"How the fuck did this happen?" I demanded. "And when?"

Jake shrugged. "Today, as far as I can tell."

I turned and stalked across the office to the window, then back again. "Eighteen months. I've been trying to buy the Lair for eighteen months and that little worm goes and sells it to Dagen?"

The Lair was another nightclub, close to Crimson. While Crimson was all about pleasure, the Lair was all about violence. Fights were hosted there nightly. It was one of the last properties in the area I didn't own. I'd already offered well above what the place was worth. I had done everything short of killing the owner and taking it. Now I wished I had.

I rubbed a hand over my hair. "He doesn't even

want the place, does he? This is just him making a move against me. Into our territory." He was like a dog pissing on a blade of grass, just because he could.

"We could blow the place up," Jake offered. "Or burn it down."

"If I thought he would care, I would," I said. "That's what he would expect us to do." I paced back and forth again.

"Sometimes it's fun to do what's expected." Jake grinned.

"Just think how many innocent people you could kill," Hutton said scathingly. He had followed us up to the office because Jake didn't trust him to stay downstairs unattended. I wasn't sure how long this was going to go on for. I either needed to hire the man or send him away. Jake didn't seem to like either option.

Jake rolled his eyes. "We wouldn't blow it up while there was anyone in there. That wouldn't be very nice."

"And you're all about being nice, you?" Hutton asked ironically.

"As a matter of fact, yes, I am," Jake said. "I'm a motherfucking saint."

I laughed. "And I'm a virgin surrounded by three wise men."

Cooper raised his hand. "I'm wise."

Jake pointed at him. "Yeah, he's wise."

"That makes one," I said. Cooper and Ben hadn't been able to get any information out of the attacker. Cooper still seemed excited after telling me about how the man screamed, and how Ben let him cut his throat. A good time was had by all.

"Figures you'd be a virgin with these two clowns around," Hutton said. He and Cooper didn't seem to have a problem with each other. They had sized each other up, exchanged nods and got on with their lives. "Want me to fix that?" He grinned.

I stopped pacing and put a hand on Jake's arm before he could pick up a sharp implement and use it on Hutton. "Are there any other properties on the market in the area right now? Has Dagen bought any others?"

"I'm looking into it," Jake said. "It could be he's been buying things quietly for a while. But the Lair, that was definitely to get our attention."

"It worked," I said sourly. I leaned against the desk and rubbed my face. "I'm guessing the knife attack was a distraction from this. He probably hoped it would succeed, but this is his real gambit."

"Oh," Cooper said suddenly. He pulled his phone out of his pocket. "I got a text from a guy offering to buy the garage." He swiped across the screen until he found what he was looking for, then showed me.

Jake looked over my shoulder. "It's half again what we offered. You should take it. That's a good price."

I turned my head to glare at him. "Have you already forgotten who the buyer is?"

Hutton snorted.

Jake glared at him. "No, I haven't forgotten. But if he keeps buying, Dagen could bankrupt himself. That would be sweet."

I shook my head. "He's not going to make the same mistake his father did." If it was that easy, I would offer him Crimson, sit back and watch the house of cards collapse. No, there was something else going on here.

"I wouldn't sell the place to him," Cooper said. "He'd probably tear it down and make it into an apartment building."

"We might do that," I said.

"Yeah." Cooper shrugged. "But if you did, at least it would be tasteful. I could do some art for it." He seemed excited by the idea.

"That can go on the 'maybe' pile," I said. An

expensive investment like that would require time and planning, and a lot of thought. It wasn't a bad idea though.

"So I should send a text back, saying no?" Cooper asked.

"No, just delete it," Jake said. "Don't give him the satisfaction of responding. That's what bullies want."

"I know." Cooper nodded. "I went to high school." He looked so sad I walked over and put my arms around him.

"Who would bully you?" I asked. "You're so sweet."

"If I give you a list, can you have them killed for me?" he asked. I wasn't sure if he was joking or not. I didn't think he knew.

That wasn't exactly how things worked though. I needed to have a better reason than that. I mean, if they beat him up…

"Make a list and I'll have Jake look into them," I told him. "Maybe you can kill one or two."

Cooper grinned. "I will, thank you."

I kissed his cheek and turned to see Hutton watching us.

"See, there's the difference between you and Dagen," he drawled. "He would have just said yes."

"I like to be fair," I said. "Killing indiscriminately

is too easy, and pisses off too many people." There was a fine line between having people scared of us, and pushing them into trying to overthrow us.

Before I could say another word, my phone rang. It wasn't my private line, it was the one I use for business. I recognised the number immediately.

I grimaced and pressed the button to answer. "Alistair Blackheart," I said with mock sweetness.

He chuckled. "Is that the best you can do, Ice Bitch?"

I snorted and rolled my eyes. "Is that the best *you* can do?" He was obviously trying to get a rise out of me, but it wasn't going to work. Not today.

"I'll leave the insults to you, Elodie" he said smoothly. "I was just ringing up to see what you thought of my gift."

Calling me names was one thing, using my real name made me want to grind my teeth.

"What is he saying?" Jake mouthed.

I pressed the button to put Dagen on speaker phone. "You shouldn't have," I said. "It must have been expensive." I wasn't sure if he was referring to the artefacts, the Lair or the would-be assassin. All of that would have cost.

"I like to think of it as an investment," he said. "In

a brighter future. One where black wolves rule, like they should."

Jake choked back a laugh.

"Isn't that a cheerful thought?" I said sarcastically. Ugh, talk about dystopia.

"I thought so." Dagen sounded smug.

"What do you really want?" I asked.

"What do any of us want?" he asked. "I want what's mine."

"Considering your family stole what you had from my family, that doesn't leave much," I remarked.

"You like to think you've won." His voice was lower, sinister. He would have intimidated a lot of people, but not me. "Neither of us started this war, but I intend to end it."

"I accept your unconditional surrender," I said sweetly. I tried to ignore Jake and Cooper giving each other a silent high-five. "Will you be retiring somewhere sunny?" A girl could hope, right?

Dagen laughed. "When I'm finished with you, you will be giving me your unconditional surrender. And your lapdog. I know he's listening."

"Hello, asshole," Jake said cheerfully. "You really should take Ivory up on her offer. It would be a lot less hassle."

"But a lot less fun," Dagen said. "Blood stains white fur so nicely, don't you think? Not to mention white hair."

Jake bared his teeth. "I prefer the way it shines off black fur, personally."

"You would know," Dagen said. "You've seen it often enough."

"That's where you're wrong," Jake said lightly. "I haven't seen it *nearly* often enough. Care to volunteer as tribute?"

"No, but I look forward to watching you die," Dagen said. "It's a bucket list thing. You know how it is."

"Right back at you," Jake said. "Nothing would give me more satisfaction."

"Hmmm, sounds as though Ivory needs to brush up on her bedroom skills." Dagen sounded impressed with himself coming up with that insult.

Cooper stood up straighter. He looked like he was going to say something in my defence.

Jake waved him back down.

"Don't give him the satisfaction," Hutton said softly.

Cooper looked like he wanted to argue, but he slumped back down and crossed his arms.

"It's not my bedroom skills you need to worry

about," I said. "It's the fact I have experience in stomping the Dagen pack back down in its place. I'm happy to do it again if you push me to it. Just remember who broke the peace if you decide to do it. The blood will be on your hands."

"I will be happy to have Ivory Claw blood on my hands," he said. "Let it rain blood."

"Did you miss your last therapy session?" I asked. "You sound a bit unhinged." He sounded dogmatic, no pun intended.

"You didn't answer my question," he said. "I know you got the artefacts. Thank you for the money, by the way. I know you bought the boy so I could get paid. And because you were panting over him like a bitch in heat."

Okay, so the last part was accurate. Could I help it if Cooper was smoking hot?

I laughed. "Jealous? Did you want him for yourself?"

Cooper made a gagging face.

"I don't need to buy fucks," Dagen said. "They come to me."

"Isn't it nice to see that some people still give to charity?" Jake said.

I put a hand over my mouth to stifle a laugh. I

could all but feel Dagen fuming at the other end of the line.

"I'm going to have to have a long think," Dagen said. "About which one of you will die first. One of you will watch the other, that's a given. Don't worry, I'll make it nice and slow. And painful."

"You must be a lot of fun at parties," Jake said dryly.

"I prefer funerals," Dagen said.

"We're happy to invite you to yours." Jake grinned. He was having way too much fun with this. "How about... This Saturday? Does that work for you?"

"I think you can die second, lapdog," Dagen said. "I would get a kick out of watching you see Ivory die."

"So, did you actually want anything, Alistair?" I asked coldly. "Or did you call to threaten us?"

"Actually I figured by now you would have heard that I bought the Lair. I just called to rub it in your face. And to see if the assassin I sent was successful. Obviously he wasn't. It seems to be a dying art these days."

I snorted at his pun. "Aren't you relieved he didn't kill me? Then you would miss out on watching me die."

"That would be a shame," he agreed. "But at least you would be out of my way."

"Sorry to disappoint you," I said. "Actually, sorry, not sorry. It wasn't even a good try. He didn't get close to me." Thanks to Hutton.

"No, but by the time you heard about the sale of the Lair, it was too late. The assassin was little more than a distraction. I didn't expect him to succeed."

"Be careful," Jake said. "All that thinking could be bad for your brain. You're not used to it."

Dagen clicked his tongue. "That was a pathetic attempt at an insult."

"That's the effect talking to you has on me," Jake said. "I feel like I have to dumb everything down."

"No," Dagen said slowly. "That's your usual level of intelligence. Did you ever wonder why my father had no use for you?"

Jake's eyes flashed dangerously. "Your father was smarter than you will ever be, which isn't saying much. He knew I would never work for him. Shame he wasn't smart enough to see a threat right in front of his face. He missed it with me and he missed it with Ivory. Then again, when it came to her, he was probably thinking with his cock. Is that why he wanted her to marry you? So he could keep her close?"

I made a disgusted face. The only thing worse than sharing a bed with one Dagen would be sharing it with two.

"He might have made a mistake, but I won't be making the same one. By the time I'm finished, there will be no way back for any white wolf." Dagen sounded certain. Not enough to worry me, but enough to know he was going to be a pain in the ass.

"You make a good threat," I said icily, "but it's going to take more than buying a nightclub and sending an inept attacker with a knife to ruffle my fur. Or some random artefacts."

He and I both knew they weren't random, but I was hoping to annoy him so that he explained the point of all of them.

"Random artefacts," he echoed. "I thought you were smarter than that. I guess I gave you too much credit."

"Maybe," I agreed. "Why don't you explain it to me?"

"Oh, I will. In time you'll understand the full meaning. And by then it will be far too late." He hung up the phone.

"That was ominous," Jake remarked. He looked unconcerned. "I always thought he should be an actor. He likes to be dramatic."

"I think he's been reading too many comic books." I put the phone down. "He's more melodramatic than dramatic."

"Can I ask something?" Cooper asked.

"Can we stop you?" Jake teased.

"I mean, I guess so." Cooper shrugged. "Have the black wolves and the white wolves ever tried to, like, make a peace treaty or something?"

I sat down on the top of the desk and crossed my legs at my knees. "My parents did. So I've been told. The black wolves responded by killing them. They never have played nice with others."

"Would you try now?" Cooper asked. "Just to save the hassle later?"

I considered the question. It was certainly a reasonable one, and something I didn't dismiss out of hand.

"If I thought he was amenable, I might," I said finally. "We have an uneasy truce right now. All he has to do is nothing and it can stay as it is. If he insists on provoking us, then all bets are off. Whatever blood is spilled after that, is on him." I cocked my head at Cooper. "I got the impression you were looking forward to spilling some blood?"

"I am," he agreed enthusiastically. "But I can do that if we don't go to war with him, can't I?"

"It sounds like you think we kill people every day," Jake remarked.

Cooper stammered. "I… I mean, not *every* day."

"Every day since you met us," I said. "But that's not normal. We don't just go around killing people for shits and giggles. In fact, Jake can go a whole month without killing someone. Maybe two months."

"It was three months one time," Jake said.

Cooper looked like he wasn't sure if we were joking or not.

"You have more restraint than Dagen," Hutton said. He toyed idly with his scar. "Some of them liked to hunt down humans just for fun. Sometimes they would kill them straight away. If there were women, they would…" He looked down at the floor. "Keep them alive a bit longer."

I didn't need him to draw me a picture to know what he was talking about. "Did you ever do that?" If he had, I would hand him over to Jake to do whatever he wanted with him. Some things were beyond forgiveness.

Hutton's head jerked up. "Rape a woman? Gods no. They didn't take us along for those hunts, they just bragged about them afterwards. Made me sick."

Plenty of paranormal people didn't think highly

of humans. It wouldn't surprise me if white wolves had hunted in the same way. Not now, unless they wanted to have their balls cut off and shoved down their throats.

I caught Jake looking at Hutton with a thoughtful expression on his face.

"What are you thinking?" I asked softly.

"Lots of things," he said. "The first is that we should go down to the Lair in the morning and have a chat with the soon-to-be former owner. Find out what Dagen offered him that made him cave. Whatever it was, we would have given him more. It must have been something really good to risk pissing us off."

I nodded. "Agreed. Although they probably bonded over the fact that they're both slimy as fuck."

Jake snapped his fingers. "I should have realised something was missing. It's our slime factor. We should have raised that."

"Personally, I prefer not to lower myself by raising something like that," I said. "If I have to be slimy, I'd rather not own the Lair. What was the second thing?"

"What we're gonna do with him." Jake nodded towards Hutton. "In case you hadn't noticed, I don't trust him."

"That has not gone unnoticed," I said. "But we could use somebody with inside knowledge of Dagen's operations."

"It's not recent knowledge," Jake pointed out.

"If it's not recent, then maybe he should be given the benefit of the doubt," I pointed out. Okay, I wasn't that naïve. Normally it took me years to trust someone. I made an exception once before, and he was standing right in front of me. Cooper seemed to be another exception, although I wasn't at the same level of trust with him as I was with Jake. Maybe I was just a good judge of people.

"I'm willing to do whatever it takes to prove myself," Hutton said.

"Which is exactly what you would say if you were trying to infiltrate our organisation," Jake said. "You should go. If we decide to give you a chance, we'll know where to find you."

Hutton nodded. He obviously knew that was the best he was going to get right now. With a heavy sigh, he slipped out the door.

"There's one more thing I'm thinking," Jake said. He cupped my cheek. "I made you a promise and I intend to keep it. All. Night. Long."

11

"Is it me, or is this place more rundown than the last time we were here?" Jake asked.

Jake lived up to every second of his promise. It was like he had nine years of pent-up sexual tension to release, or something.

Yeah, okay, I knew he had other lovers, even a girlfriend or two, but like me, they never lasted long. In his case, it didn't surprise me. He never made any attempt to hide how he felt about me. No girl likes to compete with another woman for a guy's attention, unless they have that kind of relationship. I might have agreed to share him with someone else, but he was always so focused on me, he never gave anyone a chance, not really.

Besides, I'm a hard act to follow.

"It's about the same," I said. "It *is* called the Lair. It wouldn't look right if it was fancy." I had planned to spend a shit load of money on it, and change the name. Something in keeping with Crimson, and my restaurant Scarlett. What? I like the colour red, okay?

The bouncers on the front door were hairy. I mean, *really* hairy. They looked like gorillas, with a little extra dose of human hands and face. Demons, obviously. Demons came in every form, from ones who look like giant spiders, to those who would pass as regular humans. A lot were part shifter, or part witch.

"Good afternoon," one greeted warmly. He gave me a smile like we were old friends. No doubt, he could beat the shit out of someone if he needed to.

"Good afternoon." I nodded coolly. I tried not to wince at the fact it was afternoon. Since Jake decided to take his promise literally, we didn't get to sleep until dawn. By the time I woke again, it was nearly eleven. I was usually up by ten. Half-past ten at the latest. In my line of work, late nights were standard, but I liked to get some sleep while it was dark.

The other bouncer looked nervous. "Is the boss expecting you?"

"The old boss, or the new boss?" Jake asked smoothly.

The bouncer looked like he didn't know how to answer that.

The first bouncer slapped him on the chest with the back of his hand. "The new one hasn't taken possession yet, remember? The boss has to clear out his office and all that shit." He sighed dramatically. "I so wish you'd bought the place. It would be so much better under you."

The second bouncer slapped the first back. "If you still want to have a job, don't say shit like that." His eyes shifted back and forth and he lowered his voice, "Bernie is right, though. I remember the days under Dagen. They weren't nice to demons like us. I dunno, maybe it's time for a new job." He hung his head.

"Vernon," Bernie said. "Are you really thinking of leaving? I can't imagine working here without you."

I exchanged glances with Jake.

He shrugged. "We could always use good door staff at Crimson."

Both demons' eyes widened.

"That would be amazing," Bernie said. "I've always wanted to work there. It looks so… Fancy. Especially compared to this dump."

Vernon nodded vigourously. "Shit, yeah. I'm in." He looked like he was ready to leave right now.

"You should finish your shifts first," Jake said. "And put in your notice."

"And make a list of whoever else wants to jump ship," I said. Dagen might have the Lair, but that didn't mean I couldn't steal his staff. It would be a minor annoyance to him, but I would take it. Any chance to piss him off.

Jake grinned. "Even if there is no room at Crimson, we'll find somewhere."

Bernie looked like he was ready to pee his pants with excitement. "Yes, boss. I know there's quite a few who aren't sure about sticking around."

"Good." I nodded. "So, Haigwood is cleaning out his office?"

"I would expect so, boss," Bernie agreed. "I think he is as eager to get out of here as we are."

Jake snorted.

I knew what he was thinking. He didn't need to say that Haigwood could have put the place behind him a year and a half ago.

I stepped past the bouncers and into the Lair.

The place was dark and stank of sweat and stale alcohol. Two forms sparred in the ring off to one side of the room. I had done enough self defence in the past to tell neither was enthusiastic about being there. The blows they exchanged were half-hearted at best.

On the other side of the room was a long bar. A woman around my age with hair an interesting shade of blue was talking to a man in a leather jacket who sat on a stool.

There were no other customers.

"Looks like business has gone downhill," Jake remarked. Even in the afternoon, there should be people here drinking and talking.

"Nothing puts people off like the words 'under new management,'" I remarked. "Especially when it's not us." I had my reasons for wanting the Lair, but I hadn't realised until now that I wasn't the only one who wanted me to buy the place. Or at least, anyone but Dagen.

"I'm not sure if we should be offended or not," Jake said lightly. "Shouldn't we be the most notorious ones in town?"

I responded with a brief laugh. "There's a fine line between being notorious and being a motherfucker. Alastair crossed that line a long time ago."

We walked down the corridor that led to the offices and staff area.

Sure enough, Haigwood was busy packing all of his belongings into cardboard boxes.

If I didn't know he was a demon, I wouldn't be able to tell by looking. He could pass for a normal human. One in a nicely fitting, expensive looking suit, with a stressed expression on his face.

I stood in the doorway and watched until he finally noticed me. When he did, he looked like he was going to jump out of his skin.

"Ivory. I… Didn't expect you… To drop by," he stammered.

I pressed a hand against the door frame and tapped my fingernail on the wood. "You didn't? Why is that? Perhaps you were hoping to be gone before I heard you sold the place?"

I saw from his expression that he was hoping for exactly that. Sucks to be him.

"Well." He shrugged. "I thought you might be, somewhat… Not happy. But…"

Jake crossed his arms over his chest. "Why did you do it, Haigwood? Didn't we offer you enough money? Did Dagen threaten your family?"

I looked at Jake sideways. "We did that, didn't we?"

He nodded. "Of course. Maybe we didn't go far enough."

I clicked my tongue. "That would be disappointing. You might need to step up your game."

Jake frowned. "I thought my threatening game was on point. Haigwood, where did I go wrong? Help a guy out."

Haigwood licked his lips. "Your threats were just right. Except I don't think you believed me when I said I hate my sister."

"You weren't convincing enough," Jake said. "But I meant what I said about your aunt."

"Oh I know," Haigwood said quickly. "It wasn't about the threats."

"What was it about?" I asked.

Haigwood gulped. "I owed his family a favour. They loaned me the money so I could buy this place. And they took care of some things for me. I thought they forgot about it but they didn't."

"People like that never forget," I said. I should know, I am 'people like that'. "Did it occur to you to come to me? I could have bought this place and helped you to disappear."

"He said he would find me wherever I went. And that I would still owe him a big favour. Selling him the Lair, it seemed like the best way out."

Haigwood reminded me of a snail. Slimy, and if there was any kind of disturbance, he would hide in his shell. In this case, though, I actually understood where he was coming from. I didn't like it, but I understood it. Owing someone a favour could come back and bite you on the ass, hard. That was why I made sure I never owed anyone anything, except Jake. I owed him everything in a way I could never repay.

I grimaced. "At least tell me he paid above our last offer."

Haigwood smiled slowly. "Quite a bit above, actually. He seemed very eager."

Jake chuckled. "I hope the place goes right down the toilet. That would teach him."

I smiled. If Dagen's finances imploded before Alistair did anything, that would be okay with me.

"We could turn the garage into an underground fight club," I mused. "A little competition never hurt anyone." And if it did, then it was too fucking bad.

"We could call it Ruby," Jake said. "Or Garnet."

"Or Merlot," Haigwood chimed in.

"Or just Red," I said.

"Everyone gets what they want," Haigwood said.

"Not really," I said coolly. "I didn't want to bother with having to renovate. Well, not completely."

Haigwood sighed and stopped packing. "Are you going to kill me?"

"That's a good question," Jake said. He looked at me. "Are we going to kill him?"

I thought about that for a while before I made up my mind. Then I pretended to think for a while longer. Just to make Haigwood sweat.

"You pissed me off," I told him. "Killing you might make people who keep me waiting think twice about doing that."

Haigwood looked like he was trying to figure out which way to run. Whichever way he went, it wouldn't be fast enough.

"However," I said slowly, "I'm going to let you live, because I'm in a good mood."

Haigwood looked disbelieving before he broke into a smile. "Thank you. Thank you so much. I really like not being dead. I'll finish packing and then you'll never see me again."

"I know we won't," I said. I gave him a last nod, then turned and walked down the corridor.

"Two days?" Jake asked quietly. He knew me too well.

"Make it three," I said. "Let him think he is safe. Take Cooper with you. He seems to enjoy killing almost as much as you do." I almost felt sorry for Haigwood, but he brought this on himself.

"Especially a worm like Haigwood," Jake agreed.

"The world will be a better place without people like him. And his sister could use the money."

"Make sure she gets it," I said. "And let her know that we didn't take it and why. You never know when her returning the favour might come in useful."

"Consider it done." Jake nodded.

"Have you come to wallow in your loss?" Alistair Dagen asked as we stepped back into the bar area.

"I thought I smelled something bad." Jake waved a hand in front of his face. "I thought it was just the rundown shithole we're standing in, but now I know better."

"A shithole you wanted to buy recently," Dagen pointed out. He looked me up and down like he was trying to appraise the value of a prized dog.

I tried to ignore the sudden tightness in the front of his pants. The idea of being touched by him was sickening.

Jake wiped a hand across his brow. "Thank the gods we dodged that bullet."

"God. I like the sound of that." Dagen looked smug. "You're welcome."

I snorted. "Don't flatter yourself." Ugh, he was a repulsive motherfucker.

"Oh, I don't know," Jake said. "If he was a god, it would explain why so much of the world is shit."

"You have a point," I said with a nod toward him. "Think of all the things we could blame him for.

"Here's an idea for you," Dagen said. "Maybe you should open a comedy club. You two could be the headline act."

"Only if you come and be the clown," Jake quipped.

"Wouldn't that be a circus?" I asked. I hated clowns as it was. Dagen in the role would be night-mare material.

Jake shrugged. "Close enough."

"If I was the clown, I'd be the kind who rides the dog for everyone to see." Dagen gave me a look that clearly interpreted his meaning. Not that it was particularly subtle. It made my skin crawl.

"I'm pretty sure that would be a performing monkey," Jake said. "You're not smart enough to be one of those."

Dagen's expression turned cold. "You still haven't told me what you're doing in my club."

"We were just thanking Haigwood," I said. In spite of my discomfort, the words came out as icy as always. "The price he got for this place will push up property values in the area. And since I own most of it, it seems like I'm the one to benefit the most."

In spite of what Jake said, Alistair Dagen wasn't stupid. He would have known buying the Lair would have that effect. Either that was part of his plan or something he couldn't prevent from happening.

"Seems like you owe me then, doesn't it?" he asked.

Only a punch in the dick, I thought.

I smiled sweetly. "Like hells. I don't know what you want with a dump like this anyway. Since when were you into nightclubs?" The garage was more his speed. Used-car yards. Malls. Apartment blocks.

He shrugged. "I thought I would diversify my portfolio. I wouldn't want to put all my eggs into one basket, would I now? My father made that mistake, I don't need to repeat it."

"He made a lot of mistakes," I agreed. Like ejaculating into Alistair's mother.

"Like leaving you alive and unbroken," Dagen said. "He was always a sucker for a pretty face." He narrowed his eyes at me.

"You think I'm pretty?" Jake asked. "Thanks, I'm touched."

"Tell me something." Dagen turned his gaze to Jake. "You had the money, the resources and the contacts. Why did you not take on my father your-self? Why do nothing for so many years, then hide behind her skirts?"

Jake stiffened visibly. "I wasn't doing *nothing*, I was biding my time. Waiting for someone the pack would follow. That's Ivory, if only because she has a much better ass than I do."

"Yes, she does," Dagen agreed. "But that doesn't make someone a good alpha."

"That's true," Jake admitted. "She has other qualities."

"I'm sure she does." Dagen eyed my chest.

I was starting to reconsider the wisdom of not killing him. Maybe the hassle it would cause would be worth it not to have him looking at me like I was a piece of meat.

"We should go. We have business to attend to," I said as if I thought he was just lazing around.

"Leaving so soon?" Dagen asked. "But I haven't had the fun of kicking you out yet. Or having you killed."

"That wouldn't be very hospitable," Jake said. "We didn't kill you when you were in Crimson the other night."

Maybe we should have.

"That's why I'm letting you leave," Dagen said.

There was more to it, I saw it in his shifty eyes. He was up to something, and whatever it was, it wasn't good.

"How kind of you," I said sarcastically.

"Yes it is," he agreed. He leaned in and whispered in my ear. "This time. Next time, things will be very different." His hot breath brushed my neck.

I suppressed a shudder.

He leaned back and I saw in his eyes that he was aware of his effect on me. I wanted to wipe the smug expression of his face with my fingernails. I might have tried if I didn't think he would enjoy it.

"What makes you think there will be a next time?" I asked. My ice queen façade was firmly back in place. "I can't see any reason why I would step foot back in here. Can you, Jake?"

"Nope," he agreed. "Not one." He looked like he was ready to punch Alistair in the face. Either he heard what the man said to me, or he could tell it was a threat.

Dagen clicked his tongue. "Don't be so literal. It doesn't have to be here. It could be," he spread his hands, "anywhere." He gave me a long look. It didn't take a genius to tell what he was thinking. In his mind he had me naked and on my knees. Or bent over something.

In my mind, he was lying in a pool of his own blood. I liked mine better.

I gave him an ice cold look, turned and started toward the door.

"He's a piece of work, isn't he?" Jake said once we were back outside.

"He's a piece of *shit*," I said. "I wish I knew what he was up to."

"Personally, I think he's all talk," Jake said. "He wants to rattle us. Don't give him the satisfaction."

I exhaled out my nose. "The only thing I want to give him is a one-way ticket to the seven hells. Remind me again why we don't kill him."

"Because if it's not him, it will be someone else from the Onyx Ridge pack," Jake said. "Some of them are worse."

Right now I was having a hard time picturing anything worse. "If he pushes my patience any further, I might have to change my mind. Have someone keep an eye on him. I want to know what he's doing before he even knows it."

"Someone like Hutton?" Jake asked. "He wants a chance to prove himself."

Hutton wouldn't like it, but I nodded. "Do it." Whatever it took to get one up on Alistair Dagen.

12

I WAS RIGHT, Hutton didn't like it. At first I thought he would give us a flat no. That he would walk out the door and disappear again. Hide like he had for nearly a decade.

"If I look like I'm going back, then everyone will hate my guts," he said finally. "They'll assume he," he nodded towards Jake, "is right that I'm a traitor."

"I *am* right," Jake said coldly. "That's exactly what you are. If you want a chance to convince us you can be more than that, here it is. Take it or fuck off. Better yet, Cooper over there is looking for an excuse to tear your heart out with his claws. Right, Cooper?"

Cooper cocked his head at Hutton and spoke like he was explaining why he had a favourite flavour of ice cream. "Not *specifically* your heart. Your head or throat would work too. I mean, not just yours either. People who aren't on our side in general. Y'know? It's nothing personal."

In spite of his words, I had a feeling he didn't really want to kill Hutton. The two shared the same brotherly vibe Cooper and Jake shared. He'd still do it if I asked.

"You really enjoyed killing that assassin, didn't you?" Jake asked him.

Cooper grinned. "Watching him die made me feel powerful. It was a rush. Almost as good as sex." He turned his smile on me.

Thank the gods his only sexual experience was better than killing someone. I still had it. That was gratifying to know. Better than murder. I should get that on a t-shirt.

"You're a bloodthirsty little prick," Jake said approvingly. "We have that in common."

"That and other things," Cooper said. His eyes were still on me.

"Anyway," I said. I turned to Hutton. "If you can help us, I will make it absolutely clear to everyone whose side you're on. The same will happen if I see any sign that you're planning on betraying us. You'll have more to worry about than Cooper."

Hutton nodded. "It seems like I don't have a choice."

"You don't," I agreed. "You said you would do anything. This is what we need you to do."

"Dagen is going to take some convincing that I want to work with him again," Hutton said.

"We've already put the word out there that Ivory thinks you're a traitor," Jake said. "It won't take long for it to reach him. Once he knows we rejected you, the Onyx Ridge Pack might try to contact you. The enemy of my enemy and all that."

Hutton bared his teeth at Jake. "So you already put my head on the chopping block. It's a fucking miracle I wasn't murdered on the way here."

Jake shrugged. "That was a risk I was willing to take."

"You really don't like him, do you?" Cooper asked.

"I can't think of a reason why I should," Jake said. "He's a lowlife."

"I like him," Cooper said. "Maybe you should give him a chance."

"Maybe you shouldn't be so fucking naïve, kid," Jake snarled. "You have no idea what it was like back then. You don't want to know."

"But I—" Cooper started.

"Enough," I snapped. "We have enough shit going

on without fighting amongst ourselves. The past is in the past, leave it the fuck there. Focus on the present and future. That's all that matters right now. Got it?" I looked around at all three guys.

Jake's jaw was set firm, but he nodded. "Yeah, boss. We'll play nice." As if he wasn't the one doing the provoking.

"I always play nice," Cooper said.

"This is all sorts of fucked up," Hutton said with a grunt. "Fine, I'll be your spy. Chances are, Dagen will take one look at me and have me killed. They won't forget I turned my back on them. I'm starting to think I should have stayed lost."

"No shit," Jake said. "But you didn't. Now you have to be a grown-up about the choice you made."

Hutton looked at me. "How do you put up with this asshole?" He jerked a thumb towards Jake.

"I'm starting to wonder how I put up with any of you." I watched out the office window as a small boat sailed past. It looked like a nice day on the harbour. Sometimes I wondered what it would be like to have a simple life.

Then I remembered, I would probably be bored.

"At least I'm nice," Cooper said. "You're not gonna kick me out, are you?" He actually looked worried.

"Not today," I said. "But I make no promises if you start to behave like those two."

Cooper puffed out his chest and looked smug. "I won't."

"When you're as old as us you will," Jake said. "This lifestyle leaves people bitter, twisted and fucked up. All the good things."

Hutton nodded. "None of those things are good, but the asshole is right. Pack wars leave scars."

"Are you still here?" Jake asked. "Fuck off and spy."

Hutton gave me a look like he really couldn't believe I associated with Jake, much less fucked him.

The pair were like a couple of dogs fighting over a bone. I wasn't sure I liked that analogy much. I preferred to be licked and sucked rather than chewed.

"Ben will have a phone for you," I said. "The number to contact me is programmed into it. If you get into trouble, I will do what I can. That might be nothing."

He nodded. "Understood. I can handle myself." He pointed a finger at Jake, who had opened his mouth to make some sort of smart ass comment. "I'm not talking about my cock."

"*Right.*" Jake drew the word out. "If you say so."

Hutton leaned over so he was almost nose to nose with Jake. "Not only do I say so, asshole, I'm going to be so useful to Ivory, the only one handling my cock when this is over will be her."

I raised my eyebrows at him. His absolute certainty sent butterflies fluttering through my stomach. Apparently I liked when guys got all alpha and possessive. If he proved himself, *when* he proved himself, I might just see if sex with him was better than killing. I had a feeling it would be, but the bar was pretty high.

Jake put a hand on his chest and pushed him back. "Never gonna happen, *asshole*."

"That's up to her," Hutton said. "Not you." He shot me a panty-melting smile and stalked out of the office.

"You know, he calls me asshole more than Dagen does," Jake mused.

"Dagen probably says it where you can't hear," Cooper pointed out. "I mean, you wouldn't know, would you?"

Jake shrugged. "That's true, I guess. What sort of motherfucker talks about people behind their back?"

"Isn't that what we're doing right now?" Cooper asked.

"Yeah, but it's us. And he's him." Jake pulled a

lollipop out of his pocket, took off the wrapper and stuck it in his mouth. "He deserves to be talked about."

"What the hells?" I asked him.

"Oh, sorry." He got up, walked over to a desk and opened a drawer. He pulled out an apple and tossed it to me. "I'd offer you a lollipop, but they're terrible for your teeth."

I was tempted to hurl the apple at his head, but I was hungry, so I bit into it instead. "One of these days, Jake Blakesley…"

"No one looks after you like I do," he said.

"I don't need looking after," I said darkly. "And if I want a lollipop, I'll fucking eat one."

"Do you?" he asked.

"Do I what?" I frowned at him.

"Want a lollipop," he said reasonably.

"No," I said. "But you're missing the point. I'm a grown woman, I can eat whatever I want." I knew as well as he did, that left my own devices I would probably eat whatever junk food came to hand. Still, he needed to stop treating me like I was a baby.

I finished the apple and tossed the core into the bin. "I'm going down to the gym. I need to work off some steam."

"I'll come with you," Cooper said.

"Fine." I finished scowling at Jake and turned a dazzling smile on Cooper. "If you can keep up, that is." He was obviously fit. I would be the one trying to keep up with him, but it didn't hurt to give him a challenge. Or a tease at least.

He grinned. "I can keep up. Are you coming, Jake?"

"Another time," Jake said distractedly. "I have a few things I need to deal with." He shook his head when I gave him a questioning look. "Nothing to worry about. Just tying up some loose ends and shit."

I nodded. "Okay." If he was anyone else, I would stick around until he told me what was going on. Since it was Jake, I trusted him to do what he thought needed to be done. He was probably just figuring out the best time and place to dispense of Haigwood. Those were details I didn't care to hear about. I just wanted to know when it was done.

Cooper followed me down to the gym in the basement and waited while I got changed into shorts and a t-shirt. I pulled my hair into a ponytail and tied it back with a hair tie.

"You look so cute," Cooper said when I stepped out of the changing area. He looked pretty cute himself, in shorts and a singlet. Okay, cute wasn't the right word for him. Hot as fuck comes to mind. His body was insane.

Part of me wanted to skip the workout and jump his bones. I'm sure he wouldn't have minded, but I really did need the exercise. More than just needing it, I wanted it. I liked the feeling of sweat trickling down my body after a good, hard workout session. It helped ease my stress and get my head back in the game.

Then I would jump his bones.

I sighed dramatically. "Cute? I'm a professional criminal. Head of one of the biggest criminal organisations in the country. And I get called cute." I pouted playfully.

Cooper gave me his best puppy dog eyes. "Awww, sorry." He put his arms around me and buried his face in my neck. "You're a badass, sexy, smoking hot, smart, beautiful woman."

"That's better," I said. I slid my hands around to his muscular back. Gods, was there anywhere on this guy that wasn't muscle?

"But you're also cute," he added. He tried to dodge out of the way, but I still managed to sock him on the chest.

"You're a brat," I said. "Lucky for you, you're a hot brat."

"Really?" He grinned slowly. "You think I'm hot?"

I wasn't sure if he was fishing for compliments, or really wasn't confident about his body. Fair enough, I wasn't confident at his age either. Great, now I felt old. I was only seven years older. That was barely anything. I did have a lot of life experience weighing me down though. So would he, if he stuck around me. I should push him away, but that ship sailed already. I might scare him off someday, but he was in, like it or not, for now.

"You're definitely hot," I said firmly. "I'm not in the habit of spending over a million dollars to get a guy's attention."

"I thought you just wanted to get me out of a sticky situation," he said.

"That too," I agreed. I wrapped my arms around his neck and pulled him down so I could kiss him. "I also wanted to get you *into* a sticky situation."

He chuckled against my mouth. "I didn't mind a bit." While he kissed me, he ran his hands down my body and cupped my ass cheeks. He pulled me closer to him, then reached down to hook his hands under my thighs. With what seemed like no effort at all, he picked me up until my legs were wrapped around his waist.

I already felt his erection through his shorts and mine. "We're supposed to be exercising."

"Sex is exercise," he said between kisses. He carried me a few steps to the wall and pressed my back to it. "It's good for burning calories."

I wanted to laugh and remind him Jake hardly let me eat any calories, but I didn't want to talk about that right now. I didn't want to talk about anything. Especially when he slid his hands up my shirt and cupped my breasts.

"We should really do a workout first," I said between increasingly frantic kisses.

"After." He tugged my shirt off over my head and dropped it on the ground. "I need you right now." He ground his erection into me and groaned. "Need you so bad."

After a couple of tries, he unhooked my bra and worked it down my arms. He held me firmly in place while I let go to slide the straps down over my hands.

"God, you are so beautiful," he said breathlessly. He pushed me up a little higher so he could wrap his mouth around my nipple and suck.

I pulled up the back of his shirt and pulled it over his head. He held me in place with one hand, then the other while he pulled it off. It joined my clothes on the floor.

"Are you even real?" I asked as I traced circles around his chest with my fingertips. "You feel real, but you look far too incredible." I had seen a lot of hot guys in my day, including Jake, but Cooper was... in some sort of league of his own. Or something.

He made all rational thoughts leave my brain and go straight to my hungry pussy. In the back of my mind, I knew how dangerous that was. He made me more off guard than I should be. I should be looking out for threats to my life, but instead I was too busy thinking about getting his cock into me as soon as possible.

He chuckled. "I was going to," he licked my other nipple, "say the same about you. My cock has never been so hard, and I'm nineteen—nearly twenty."

Reminding me how young he was made me feel like a predator. But I was a criminal and a wolf, so predator came with the territory. At least he wasn't underage.

He lowered me to my feet just long enough to yank off my shorts and panties. I helped him out of his just as quickly.

He picked me up again and held me there with

one hand while with his other, he positioned his cock outside the entrance to my pussy. He teased me for a while, brushing against my clit, then rubbing more firmly until I was panting and wet.

I groaned. "Please. I need you inside me."

"Soon." He was almost as breathless with need. "You're going to wait until I'm ready."

Gods, that was hot. I liked that he wanted to take control. As long as it didn't spill over into our work life.

I rubbed against him and tried to push my pussy onto his cock. I only had so much patience at the best of times.

"Not yet," he scolded. "And don't come either. Not till I tell you to."

"You suck," I said playfully. "You need it as much as I do."

"More," he said. "I laid awake all night listening to you and Jake. I got myself off once or twice, but it's not as good as this."

Okay, so the idea of him listening and touching himself made me melt a little further.

"We should all play together some time," I said. Oh yeah, I would *happily* be the meat in a Jake and Cooper sandwich. Bring it on.

"Yes please," he said. He slid his cock over my clit. His tip was already slick with precum.

"Coop Wheeler, if you don't fuck me..." I growled.

"What will you do?" he asked teasingly. He let go of his cock and grabbed both of my wrists in one hand. He raised them above my head and pinned them to the wall. He locked his gaze on mine.

I saw no sign in there of a naïve young man. Instead, he was confident, dominant. Determined that I would play by his rules. This was different from Jake's possessive, alpha dominance. This was a young wolf asserting himself.

It was sexy as fuck.

"I'll wait until you're ready to fuck me," I said. I wasn't meek, not for a moment. It was not a battle of wills, because I would have won that. It was a compromise. I would let him have this moment, in return for many others.

"Hells yeah," he said. He drove himself into me, hard. So hard I almost screamed and came on the spot.

I saw a flicker of hesitation on his face, concerned that he'd hurt me. In the next second, it was gone. He pounded relentlessly, hard, fast and firm.

Pinned as I was to the wall, all I could do was match his rhythm as best I could. I rolled my hips and adjusted so he could slam in deeper.

"Ivory," he said breathlessly. "You are... Everything."

"Hells yeah, I am," I agreed breathlessly. "Don't you forget it."

"I will never forget it," he said firmly. "I could never forget you." He gritted his teeth and ground his balls against the entrance to my pussy. "Fuck yeah."

He paused for a moment to slam his lips into mine. His kiss was as furious as his thrusts. His tongue pushed deep into my mouth, almost to the back of my throat.

I sucked on it like it was his cock.

"Mmmm." He simultaneously thrust into my mouth and my pussy.

It made me lightheaded and more aroused than ever.

He broke off the kiss long enough to say, "Come for me."

I couldn't have waited a second longer anyway. I came so fiercely it was almost painful. Wonderful, beautiful pain that filled every part of me and made my pulse spike better than any adrenaline rush.

He followed me half a second later. His grunts and groans filled the gym better than any exercise class. His hand tightened around my wrists, and he pressed me more firmly against the wall. He drove in with harder strokes like his life depended on it.

He let out a deep, guttural growl from the back of his throat. If he was in wolf form, he probably would have howled.

I cried out with him. My breath came in hard pants that got softer and softer as I came down from my high.

"Oh. My. Gods," he said. "Sex is way better than I ever imagined. Or maybe it's just you."

I laughed softly. "It's definitely just me," I joked.

He kissed me lightly. "That sounds accurate. Because you're pretty fucking epic. Now, we should do a workout."

I made a face. I had forgotten about that. "I guess we should." A lot of my frustration at dealing with Dagen was gone, but there was still some left in the back of my mind. Probably more than just a workout was going to eradicate, but it was a start.

13

"GOOD WORKOUT?" Jake asked as I stepped back into the office, Cooper at my heels. He peered at us over the rim of his reading glasses. It was clear from his expression he knew more than a workout went on. Or at least he suspected.

"Have you got a camera down there?" I slipped into a chair behind my computer and raised my eyebrows at him.

He grinned. "We have cameras everywhere. For security purposes, of course."

I snorted. "Of course." I had no intention, or need, to apologise for anything he saw when he was spying on me.

Cooper smiled and settled into a chair. "I'd like to see the footage if you recorded it."

"As it happens, I did," Jake said. "We can watch it later with some popcorn."

I opened my laptop and logged on. "What else have you been doing? Anything useful?" I rolled my eyes at him, but he just grinned back.

"Just running background checks on the Lair's staff. Most of them are demons, but a couple are witches. Some are actually human. One or two are shifters."

I nodded and tapped at my keyboard. "I can't help thinking Dagen buying the Lair didn't happen in isolation. He also made an offer on the garage." I nodded towards Cooper. "We always keep a close eye on anything that comes up for sale, whether we want to buy it or not, but I feel like we missed something."

I brought up files on the real estate listings and sales for the last two to three years.

"We would have noticed a pattern," Jake said.

"Only if it was obvious," I said. "He bought the Lair under Black Wolf Holdings. He wanted us to notice that." Anything I bought legally was purchased under White Wolf, unless it was shady. That stuff was under Ivory Claw, or one of my smaller companies.

"I'll help you look." Cooper pulled a chair over

closer. Close enough that our shoulders touched. "What are we looking for, exactly?"

"I'm not sure," I admitted. "Something so subtle it was easily missed."

Cooper peered at the screen. "Is Dagen's name really Dagen?"

"Yes, why?" I asked.

"Well, your real name isn't Ivory? Is it?" Cooper asked. "And your last name isn't Claw."

I smiled. "Are you sure about that?"

He blinked a couple of times. "I'm pretty sure."

"It's not," I assured him. "But as far as I know Dagen is his name. Although, Asshole suits him better."

Cooper grinned. His smile faded and he pointed at the screen. "Someone named Tony Jones bought a hairdressing salon down the street. He also bought a computer repair shop. No one is going to look twice at a bunch of technology coming in and out. Have you had a problem with hackers?"

Jake's head jerked up. He looked outraged. "We have professional hackers on the payroll to prevent other hackers from hacking us."

"Say that three times fast." Cooper chuckled.

I laughed softly. "His point is, they won't get in

here. That doesn't mean they haven't tried." I looked over to Jake.

He nodded. "I'll look into it." He seemed certain he wouldn't find anything. It was his job to know if they had, as much as it was mine.

"Has this Tony Jones bought anything else?" I said, half under my breath.

"I don't know, but don't you think Tony Jones is a good name for a gangster?" Cooper said. He seemed to like the idea.

"It's not as good as mine," I said distractedly. I was checking out every name on the list now.

"Can I ask you a question?" Cooper asked.

"Yeah, what?" I said.

"What is your real name?" he asked.

I hesitated. I glanced over at Jake, who shrugged. I had gone by Ivory for so long, I only thought about my birth name when Jake or Asshole called me that. It wasn't so much a secret as just… not me anymore. And it was an intimate thing between Jake and I.

"Hey look, here's another one," Cooper said before I could respond to his question. "Two and a half years ago, Tony Jones bought a newspaper stand. All the better to spy on us with?"

"Well spotted," I agreed.

"Should we go and talk to this Tony Jones guy?" Cooper asked. He looked like he was ready to jump up and down in this chair.

"Settle down, Murder Puppy," Jake said. "Let me see what I can find on this guy first."

Cooper sat back. "There might be more."

We kept on looking, but the only other people who appeared to have bought more than one property was us.

"Why a hairdressing salon?" I said finally.

"It looks harmless?" Cooper suggested.

"Like you," I teased.

He grinned. "Exactly." He leaned in to plant a lingering kiss on my mouth. "On the outside, I look like a nice guy. On the inside I'm—"

"A murder puppy," I finished for him.

"Is that my nickname?" He didn't seem bothered by that. "Ivory and the Murder Puppy. I like the sound of that. What is Jake's nickname?"

"The only people who give me nicknames are my enemies," Jake said without looking up from his screen.

"They're your enemies because they give you nicknames, or only your enemies give them to you?" Cooper asked teasingly.

"Both," Jake said. "Would it surprise you to learn this Tony Jones doesn't seem to exist?"

"I'm shocked," I said sarcastically. "How many other people who bought real estate in the area in the last few years also didn't exist?"

"Apart from us?" Jake quirked an eyebrow at me. "I'm guessing the number is higher than zero. I'll look into it."

I nodded. "Go back as far as you can. We don't know how long this has been going on." We should have suspected it, but the uneasy peace seemed to have kept Dagen in his box for the most part. My father used to say 'complacency is your enemy.' He was right about that. He was a very good example of where complacency got you. In his case, it was with his brains spread across the wall.

"If Tony Jones doesn't exist, then can we go and talk to him?" Cooper asked.

"I feel like that sentence shouldn't make any sense," I said. "I think it would be a good idea to go and take a personal look at his establishments."

"I wish he owned a bakery, or a donut shop." Jake stretched his arms over his head. "I could use some sugar right now."

"You'll have to settle for a trim," I told him dryly. Now that he mentioned sugar, I would kill for one of those custard and apple filled pastry things. Jake couldn't even object to it, since apples were a fruit. At this point, if he objected, he might get a pie to the face, courtesy of my hand. Knowing him, he'd wipe it off and eat it. Also knowing him, he would prefer to cream pie my pussy than have me cream pie his face.

"Newspaper stands usually sell snack food," Cooper said helpfully.

"Let's go there first," Jake said quickly. He opened the drawer beside him.

"If you're about to pull out an apple and give it to me, I'm gonna stuff it up your ass," I growled.

He closed the drawer again.

"If I had a drawer, I would keep jelly beans in there for you," Cooper said. "Do you like the black ones?"

I grimaced. "No. Yuck. I like the red ones and the white ones. And the purple ones. But if you did that, Jake would eat them all."

"Only to save you from all that sugar," Jake protested. "Not all heroes wear capes."

"Some of them are going to wear their face on the back of their heads if they don't back the fuck off," I said with mock sweetness.

"I'd like to see that." Cooper grinned.

Jake narrowed his eyes at him. "Who the fuck's side are you on, Murder Puppy?"

"Hers," Cooper said without missing a beat. "I'm sorry but you've seen her ass."

"Many times," Jake agreed. "I never get tired of seeing it. But mine is pretty impressive too, don't you think?"

"Of course," Cooper agreed. "But if yours is a ten, hers is a fifteen. I'm sorry, that's just the way I see it. Besides, she's the boss."

"Exactly," I said. "Always take the boss's side, regardless of the awesomeness of their ass."

"But an awesome ass doesn't hurt," Jake said.

"No it doesn't," I agreed. "Right then, let's go to this newsstand. I have a sudden need to satisfy my craving for jellybeans. And maybe get a magazine."

Did they even sell those at newsstands anymore? So much was digital these days, newsstands probably sold more snacks and bus tickets than papers.

"We should take Ben along with us too," Jake said. "With Dagen sniffing around, I'd rather be safe than conspicuous."

I considered that for a moment. I would rather be both. Nothing says 'look at me.' like walking down the street with three hot guys.

"Can you ever be inconspicuous?" Cooper asked.

He watched me as I stood. "I don't know about anyone else, but I can't take my eyes off you when you walk into a room."

The feeling was entirely mutual.

"You're right, she can't," Jake said. "But that's the image she's spent years building. When she walks into a room, people pay attention. It's great until she wants to sneak around."

"Maybe I should wear a wig," I said dryly. "No one would recognise me as a redhead."

"I still would," Jake said. "I would recognise you anywhere. You could change everything about you and you would still have the presence to make people notice you. So maybe you should sit this one out. Let the pup sniff around."

I considered it for a moment. Finally, I shook my head. "No. I want Asshole to know we're sniffing around. Let him know we're onto his bullshit. Besides, the mysterious Tony Jones might not have anything to do with Dagen. He might be a regular, old human criminal. Or a front for someone else. If anyone else is trying to muscle in on my territory, they better know we're coming for them."

"And then they'll have their face on the other side of their head?" Cooper asked hopefully.

"Exactly," I agreed. I didn't know how I would do that, but it sounded like fun.

I led the way to the door and nodded for Ben to follow us. He looked at me and the other guys with a brief, but intense look. I could almost see him wondering where this left us and our occasional hookups. Truthfully, I didn't know. We'd known each other as long as Jake and I. Jake actually hired him to guard me after the auction. There was little about me he didn't know. And the man knew what to do with his tongue.

The question was, how complicated did I really need my life to be? That was yet another question for later. In the meantime, I offered him a smile. He responded with a faint one back, and a nod. He was never anything but professional when other people were around.

I rode the elevator down to the bottom of the building with a car full of testosterone. The smell was delicious. For a solid minute, I considered pressing the stop button and seeing how many orgasms I could have before someone tried to get us out. If we weren't on business, I might have. Besides, Jake and Cooper agreed to share, but Ben was a whole other conversation. One I wasn't ready for yet.

The newsstand was only two blocks down the street, so we walked. Jake took his place beside me, his hand on my back, while the other two guys walked in front and behind. We absolutely didn't go unnoticed. In fact, several people, men and women, stopped to gape at Cooper. And he said *I* wasn't conspicuous. Even with clothes on, he was a walking bag of sex. A human boner. A wet dream. A... You get it.

The gods knew Jake was just as hot, but in a dangerous, coiled aggression kind of way. No one would ever mistake him for someone who was harmless.

Ben—he looked like a bodyguard, with his dark trousers and vigilant, intense gaze. If there was something out of place, he'd notice it.

If the woman who worked at the newsstand was spying on us for Dagen, I would eat my left Louboutin. She looked younger than Cooper and smelled of pure human. And anxiety.

"Can... Can I help you?" she asked. "I'm sorry, this is only my second day. The guy who was here quit suddenly. I'm still trying to figure everything out."

I exchanged glances with Jake. No, that didn't sound suspicious at all.

"That's unfortunate," I told her. "I quite liked," I frowned, "what was his name?"

"Jason," the woman said. "Apparently he had some family stuff to deal with."

I nodded. "Jason. Of course. Well, I hope everything is okay with him. In the meantime, do you have any jelly beans?" I saw them the moment I walked up, but it didn't hurt to let her serve me. If I was nice, she would remember me, and she might come in useful someday. Or Dagen was using her and she would end up floating in the harbour in a day or two. Either way, I wasn't going to lose any sleep over it.

She pointed me to them and then moved over to serve another customer.

I grabbed a packet or two and ignored the look Jake gave me. "If you want some, you better buy your own," I told him.

He grabbed a couple but frowned around at the stand. "I have a feeling we need to get the fuck out of here."

His words and tone made the hair on the back of my neck stand up. Whatever vibe he caught, I caught it too now.

"Yeah," Ben said softly. He frowned, like he

couldn't put his finger on what was up. If he was on edge, then so was I.

I nodded and placed the jelly beans on the counter in the centre of the stand. Jake added another two packets and three packets of corn chips. When I raised my eyebrows at him, he added three packets of salt and vinegar chips to the pile.

"Are you going to let me eat some of that?" I asked.

He leaned in to whisper in my ear. "I'm going to eat all the jelly beans and make my cum so sweet you won't be able to stop drinking it."

"The hells you are," I said. I was absolutely eating some of it. And his cum. I paid for everything and picked up my jellybeans and a bag of each of the chips. "Besides, it's tasty enough as it is." I gave him a smile, but I doubted anyone who was paying attention would miss the edge in my expression. I wanted to get away from here as quickly as possible.

"Come on, Pup," Jake said to Cooper. "We're stocked up on crap food for a while." He spoke lightly, but I knew that expression on his face. Every nerve in his body was on alert. He didn't know what he was looking for, but he knew he was looking for something. Call it wolf instincts, or too many years of having to watch our backs, but he sensed something. He appeared as unnerved as Ben.

"What is that?" Cooper asked after we took a few steps away. "There's a weird smell in the air."

Jake swung his head around to stare at Cooper, then sniffed. "Fuck, you're right. The hells is it?"

I sniffed and shook my head. "It smells like rotting fruit." I turned my head. "And it seems to be coming from—"

I looked directly at the newsstand as it was blasted to smithereens.

14

ALL THREE OF the guys shoved me to the ground and threw themselves around me to shield me from the blast. They were lucky they didn't slam me face first into the ground. Getting injured in the explosion would be the least of their troubles if I broke my nose.

Instead, I ended up on my knees, my head down over them, arms over my face.

The explosion went on for what seemed like days. In reality, it was only a matter of seconds. Terrifying seconds in which I was almost sure I was about to die. I was going to end up in chunks like my parents had. No one would ever know it was me, because I made sure to have anything that would identify me erased from any databases anywhere in the world.

The worst part was, I didn't get to eat my jelly beans first. Yeah, okay, weird things cross your mind when you're sure you're going to die.

I slowly became aware the world had fallen still. My ears were ringing. It filtered out the sound of screaming and then the sound of sirens approaching the area.

"Ivory?" I realised Jake had said my name several times already. "Ivory? El?"

Gradually, I worked my way out of my state of shock. I blinked a few times and shook my head.

"I'm okay." I let him help me to my feet and looked around.

Where the newsstand was, only now a smouldering mess of metal and the remains of the woman who worked there were left. Several people lay close by, dead or badly injured.

"Shit," Cooper said softly. He had a gash on his cheek from where something hit him, but he otherwise looked okay.

Ben staggered to his feet with Jake's help and rubbed the back of his head. His hand came away red with blood, but he waved Jake off. "It's just a graze." He must have tried to shield all of us. He was incredibly lucky he wasn't killed as well. Was it wrong that I found that incredibly hot?

"Should we get out of here?" Cooper asked.

The sirens were getting closer.

"Can you walk?" Jake asked me.

"Yeah. I'm fine." I practically had a brick wall of guys between me and the blast. I was pissed off, but not hurt. I would have been even more pissed off if any of us died.

Jake grabbed my hand and led me away at a slow walk, while people came running from the buildings around us.

"That was too fucking close," Jake growled. "If the motherfucker wants a war, then he's going to fucking get one."

"Lucky we didn't go for a haircut," I said.

Jake snorted his agreement.

"This is all kinds of fucked up," Cooper said. He looked a little dazed. He stopped and looked back at the carnage.

I dropped back slightly to talk to Ben. "Do you need to see a paramedic?"

He shook his head slowly. "No. I'm fine, boss. Thanks. I'll have a headache later, but no harm done otherwise." The back of his hair was matted with blood, but if he said he was okay, I had no choice but to believe him.

"That was badass," I said softly. I reached for his hand—the one not covered in blood, and gave it a squeeze.

He squeezed back and offered me a faint smile. "I try to be a badass as often as I can. I like that you noticed." The look he gave me went beyond professional. I suspected my return gaze did as well. If he died, I'd be more than pissed. It's funny how you don't really see what's in front of you until it's almost gone. Hells, why not complicate life a bit more? Our time on this planet was too short not to take risks.

"I always notice," I assured him. I realised I was still holding his hand and let it go. I caught Jake's glance, but he looked unworried. He was used to there being something between Ben and I. He might have assumed it would go further some day. As long as I didn't lock him out again, he was okay with it.

I turned my attention to Cooper, who was still glassy eyed. "Are you all right?"

He blinked. "Yeah, I guess. Just… This death thing doesn't seem like so much fun when it's almost you."

I snorted softly. "No. It really isn't. I would have to suggest he knows we're onto him now." Dagen must have realised we would go looking in the database once we heard about him buying the Lair. That, or someone told him we were coming.

"This is bullshit," Jake growled.

"It is," I agreed. "But at least we got out alive."

"Thank the gods for that but…" He waved a hand back toward the mangled newsstand. "We were supposed to do that. We're supposed to blow up *his* shit. He's not supposed to blow up his own shit to kill us. Who does that? It's fucked up."

I stopped and looked up at him. "You're pissed because he blew up his own property, and you missed out on doing it?"

He looked like he was struggling to deny it. "A little bit," he admitted. "But mostly it's because he could have killed us. He could have killed *you*."

"Pfft, I'm not that easy to kill," I said lightly. "He's tried twice now in two days and I'm still standing."

"It's the first bit I'm worried about." Jake ran a hand over his head. "He's tried to kill you. He's not going to go to all this effort and then just give up because he didn't succeed the first two times. He'll keep coming until he succeeds. Or we get to him first."

"At least he stopped me from eating those jelly beans," I pointed out.

Jake looked like he didn't know if he should be angry, or laugh in response to that. "I would prefer you to eat crap food than get blown up." He exhaled hard out his nose like an angry, fire breathing dragon. It was kinda sexy, seeing him like this. Furious, but alive. Especially the alive part. I'm fucked up, but I'm not that fucked up.

"Does that mean you're going to lay off on what I eat?" I asked.

"Nope," he said lightly, but immediately. "You might need to outrun him someday. Eating jelly beans would make it that much harder to do."

"Spoilsport," I teased.

"I still have mine." Cooper's hand trembled, but he held out a bag of jelly beans and one of chips.

"Shit gets blown up, but you hold on to the food?" Jake asked, disbelieving.

Cooper shrugged. "I guess I had them in my fist." They were both somewhat crushed, but more or less intact. "I'm not hungry anymore." He held them out to me, but Jake grabbed them first and dropped them in a bin as we walked past.

"We need a proper meal after this," he said firmly. "All of us. Maybe steak."

"I could eat steak," I agreed. Like Cooper, I wasn't actually hungry either.

"Me too," Ben agreed. He touched his head again, but the blood seemed to have dried already. That was fortunate. I would have insisted he see a witch otherwise. I might anyway. We couldn't risk losing him just because of the way he felt about them.

"I guess I could try one," Cooper agreed.

"Good." Jake patted him on the shoulder. "Besides, Ivory is going to need another shower and change of clothes."

I looked at myself and grimaced. My nice white blouse was now streaked with dirt and the gods knew what else. My skirt had a tear in it from where I'd fallen to my knees. My hair was probably a mess. On the up side, my shoes looked undamaged.

That was a win.

They wouldn't stay that way very long if I saw Alistair Dagen in the next five minutes. I would probably stab my heels into his skull. Why not? My blouse was already messy, it might as well have blood and brains on it too.

"I feel like I spend half my life in this shower these days," I said. "And the other half ordering new clothes."

"What part about that are you objecting to?" Jake asked.

"Neither of them," I replied. "I was just saying, that's all."

"The shower seems like a good place for you." He gave me a steady look. "You might be safer in there."

"And a lot more naked," Cooper said. Apparently he recovered from his shock. There was nothing like talking about, or thinking about sex to make someone recover quickly. Especially a guy. Okay, and especially me. And all the other women in those delicious groups on social media. And…

Okay, it's pretty universal.

Ben smiled, but he didn't disagree.

"You guys are not going to put me in a box for the rest of my life to keep me safe," I said firmly.

"Actually, I was going to stay in the shower with you," Jake said. "To keep me safe. You'll protect me, right?" He wiggled his brows.

"Me too," Cooper said. He frowned briefly, then added, "What is El short for?" He looked from me to Jake and back again. "I heard him call you that."

The side of my mouth drew back. "It's short for Elodie. That's the name I was born with."

He smiled. "That's pretty." After a moment, he added, "Can I keep calling you Ivory? It sounds so badass."

I smiled back at him. "Please do. Especially in

front of other people." I gave Jake a meaningful glance.

He shrugged. "I didn't think anyone was listening. And I was worried about you. And you were going to tell him sooner or later. And Ben already knows."

"I guess so," I agreed.

"I feel like I just got membership into some exclusive club," Cooper said. He looked awed.

Sometimes he was so fucking cute I couldn't believe it.

I laughed softly. "You got that the moment I won your auction. And let me fuck you." The connection I had with the guy was so damn strong it was almost scary. Especially since we'd known each other for a handful of days. The bond I had with Jake grew over time, and was irreplaceable, but this was no less real. And Ben… That was something I needed to think about later. And then there was Hutton.

All of this thinking about guys and relationships was starting to make my body throb with heat. Nothing would ever be simple again, would it?

"We should hurry," Jake said. "I don't know about you three, but I'm not in the mood to answer questions from the cops."

I wasn't worried about the police. They either worked for me or wouldn't believe me if I told them about Dagen. Either way, talking to them would be a waste of time.

"See if you can slip them some evidence or something," I said. "I doubt they'll figure it out before he tries something else." People like him and me were too good at covering their tracks. It was what we did. Sometimes I felt sorry for the cops assigned to cases like this. Many of them were decent, hardworking people. Many were paranormal like us. They knew they would never get to the bottom of this, no matter how hard they tried. And the innocent people caught up in it... That blood was on Dagen's hands.

"I'm guessing the guy who quit two days ago wasn't a coincidence," Cooper said. "I mean, that would be the mother of all coincidences. Right?"

"Coincidences are usually as real as Santa," Jake said dryly. "He's probably disappeared off the face of the planet. Either voluntarily or not so much."

"We can try to track him down when the dust settles," I said. The people in the shops and offices nearby should at least have some idea what he looked like. They wouldn't be much help right now though, not with police and ambulances crawling around the area.

"Would it be a good idea to check if the hairdresser or the computer place had a sudden change in staff?" Cooper asked.

"Absolutely it would," I agreed. "If I was the type to gamble, I would bet on it." I wasn't a gambler though. Everything I did was careful and deliberate. Okay, most things. I could be spontaneous from time to time. It helped to keep people on their toes.

"Do you want me to go and ask?" Cooper asked.

"No," Jake replied. "They know who you are by now. We'll send someone they don't know. But not yet. That's the first thing they'll be expecting us to do."

"So they'd probably have someone waiting for us," Cooper said. "Unless this Dagen asshole likes blowing shit up."

"Generally speaking, blowing up your own businesses is bad *for* business," Jake said. "I don't think he would make a habit of it."

"Right," Cooper said slowly. "They probably figured the newsstand would be the most likely place we would turn up. For all the reasons why we went there first. And destroying that causes minimal damage to everyone and everything. I mean, what's a handful of dead humans?"

"That's about right," I agreed. Dagen wouldn't

give a crap about collateral damage. Whatever it took to get to us. To get to me.

I hurried my steps as we approached Crimson. Partly because I felt exposed after the explosion. And partly because I looked like shit. The guys might get away with looking rough and dirty, but with me, it wouldn't go unnoticed. All right, lately it was becoming a more regular occurrence to see me with blood or juice, or whatever all over me. I didn't want it to become a habit.

"So when Jake said we were supposed to blow up Dagen's shit," Cooper said slowly. "A few dead humans happen then too?"

"You got a problem with that?" Jake asked.

A frown flashed across Cooper's forehead. "No. I was just wondering, that's all."

"We try to avoid unnecessary carnage," I said. "I'm not a fan of bombs, arson, shooting rampages, forcing trains off the tracks, bringing down aeroplanes, stuff like that. I prefer the personal touch of having people killed face-to-face. Or by an assassin if I have to."

"Can you send one of those after Dagen?" Cooper asked. "I mean, he tried."

"If you can call that guy an assassin." Jake curled his lip. "He was about as stealthy as..." He thought for a moment. "Throwing an elephant off a rooftop."

Cooper and I both laughed.

Then Cooper asked, "We don't do that, right?"

Jake stared at him in disbelief for a moment, then started laughing so hard tears rolled down his cheeks. "Do we... Throw elephants... Off..." He slapped his thigh.

His laughter was infectious. I smiled and patted Cooper on the shoulder as we headed through the private door and into Crimson.

"Jake laughs now, but he hasn't seen my to-do list," I joked. "The next item on it is throwing a giant animal off the roof."

"Only if it's a big, black wolf," Jake said between laughs. "Or even a small one."

I snapped my fingers. "I should have invited Alistair Dagen up to the helipad the other night." Not that he would be stupid enough to go up there with me. That would be far too easy.

"There's a helipad?" Cooper asked. "Can I see?" He looked like a little boy eager to open Christmas presents early.

"After I get clean," I said firmly.

He looked disappointed for a moment but then said, "So, can we send an assassin after Dagen?"

Jake gave him the side eye. "Are you volunteering?"

Cooper's mouth opened and shut a couple of times.

I decided to put him out of his misery. "Being an assassin takes years of training. Usually they have to learn to be stealthy and careful. Sneak in, sneak out. If you want to do the training, I can sponsor you, but I hope Dagen is long dead before you finish it."

Cooper gaped at me. "Me? An assassin? That would be fucking awesome." If he looked like a boy at Christmas before, now he looked like several Christmases, half a dozen Easters and a fistful of wet dreams.

"Wouldn't hurt to have a few more on the payroll," Jake said. "I have a feeling you'll be good at it, Murder Puppy. Just imagine, you get to kill bad guys for a living."

Cooper grinned.

That, right there, is a very good reason why he would make one hells of an assassin. No one would see a guy who looked like him coming, until it was far too late.

"Then you could come home and draw a picture of your victims," Jake said cheerfully.

I shook my head at him. "That is some fucked up

shit right there. Also, no, don't do that because that's evidence."

Cooper looked slightly disappointed, but he nodded. "Yeah, okay I won't do that."

"And in answer to your question," I said, "I haven't ruled out sending an assassin after Dagen. Right now though, it would be obvious who sent it. He might be trying to provoke a war, but we aren't there yet."

Jake looked like he wanted to argue, but I gave him a firm look.

"He has his toe on the line, but he hasn't crossed it. None of us died, and he hasn't blown up anything we own. Until he does, then we just keep doing what we're doing, and be careful."

"Fine," Jake said. "But if he sticks his toenail over, I'm going to chop it off. And his toe. And then the rest of him."

"Get in line," I told him.

Jake looked thoughtful. "I'm a wolf, I don't really do 'getting in line.' How about we do it as a pack?"

"Works for me," I agreed.

The elevator doors slid open to the tenth floor. Ben stepped out first, eyes cautious, vigilant.

I waited until he signalled that it was safe. It should be, it wasn't that easy for anyone but us to get up here, but we know what complacency can do. Right?

"Stay out here," Jake told him. "No one goes up or down without my say-so. I'll arrange for a witch to look at your head."

Before Ben could do more than nod and look slightly irritated, Jake ushered the rest of us into my apartment.

"I'm going to have a shower." I unbuttoned my blouse and let it slip down my arms and onto the floor.

"I have a better idea." Jake grabbed my hand and drew me to him. "How about I get you messier before you get clean?" He pressed his mouth to mine in a demanding kiss.

I felt the hooks of my bra release, but it took me a moment to realise it was Cooper who did it. He pulled my bra down off my arms and slid his arms around me from behind. He ran his hands up my belly slowly, then started to knead my breasts.

I leaned back against him, taking Jake with me.

"I think she likes the idea," Cooper said.

Jake pulled his head back and gave me a smouldering look with his dark eyes. "Good, because neither of us was asking."

Holy fuck

That sent a shiver up desire down to my core.

Cooper leaned around to kiss the side of my neck. "Nope, we're not. We're wolves. We take what we want."

That was one way to ruin a perfectly good pair of panties.

While Cooper started taking off my skirt, Jake ran his tongue around my lips and down my cheek to my neck.

I groaned softly. My body ached, but they kept their touches light except when they both grabbed the top of my panties and ripped them. They ended up with about half each.

Jake pressed his erection to the front of my leg, and Cooper into the back. It was all I could do not to beg one of them to stick a cock *somewhere*.

"Your bedroom, *now*," Jake ordered.

I had no words. All I could do was nod and do as he said. Both guys stripped on the way, leaving a trail of clothes on the floor. By the time they manoeuvred me onto the top of the covers, they were both naked.

Gods burn my soul, I wanted them both so badly. They couldn't be more different from each other, but they were both as sexy as hells.

Jake traced around my lips with the tip of his

finger. "Open for me." He lay beside me, so close all I could see was his flat stomach and rock hard cock.

I opened my mouth and let him slide his cock inside my mouth.

"You can take more than that," he said. He pushed himself all the way to the back of my throat.

I tried not to gag, but he put a hand on the back of my head to keep me from pulling away. I was used to being in control. Used to taking a guy in as deep as I wanted. This was different. Letting go was difficult, but I wanted to. Needed to.

He pulled halfway out and pushed in just as deep. "Good girl."

I raised my eyebrows at him, but he only smirked in response.

Cooper hooked my legs over his shoulders and settled his face down between my thighs. There was nothing stealthy about the way his tongue went to work on me. He lapped at my folds and my clit like he'd been doing it for years. His hands slid under my hips to firmly grip my ass.

With him working my pussy, and Jake fucking my throat, I was on the verge of coming in only a minute or two. I sucked hard and bucked gently in rhythm.

"Don't let her come," Jake said to Cooper. "*We* decide when that happens."

Cooper made a sound of agreement and pulled his face back.

I made a sound of *dis*agreement, like a growl in the back of my throat. The noise was cut off by Jake ramming his cock harder into my mouth. I did gag this time, but then he slid out of me and patted my head like I was a dog.

"Roll her over," Jake said. To me, he said, "Straddle him." He reached into the draw beside my bed and pulled out some lube. Trust him to know where I kept it.

Cooper lay on his back. He gripped my hips and lowered me slowly onto his cock. "Mmm, hells yeah. Have I mentioned lately that your pussy is amazing?"

"Not lately, no," I said. "Your cock is pretty amazing too." I rolled my hips and rubbed my clit as I rode him. I closed my eyes and breathed hard out my nose.

Jake knelt behind me and bent me forward. He reached around and lightly gripped my throat. "No coming until we say so. Understood?"

I murmured to let him know I understood.

Apparently that wasn't enough. He tightened his grip slightly.

"Say it."

"I understand," I said between already ragged breaths.

"Good." He let go of my throat and unscrewed the cap of the lube. He squeezed out a finger full and rubbed it all over my rear hole. He tossed the tube aside and positioned his cock outside my entrance. Slowly and gently, he eased himself inside.

"Don't tense," he said.

I swallowed hard and nodded. I was trying not to, but the feeling of two cocks inside me at the same time made me feel so full I thought I might burst. In the best way possible.

He gradually pushed himself deeper, giving me time to adjust each time. Finally, he slid all the way in and started to thrust slowly. He put his hands on my hips and guided me to keep rising and falling while he stayed inside me.

"Holy gods," Cooper whispered. "I can feel you both."

Of course, there wasn't much more than skin and muscle between my ass and my pussy. They must be bumping tips with each thrust.

Holy.

Fucking.

Hotness.

I couldn't decide what turned me on more, this, or if they touched each other directly. I decided to call it a tie and closed my eyes to enjoy every feeling, every sensation they sent through me.

After a moment or two, the three of us had a rhythm going like we practised this every day. Maybe we should.

Desire rose like a relentless tide, bearing down on me and threatening to wash me away.

"I need to come, please," I said. Gods, I was begging. Only two people in the world would ever make me beg, and they were both fucking my holes right now.

"Not yet," Jake said.

Cooper smiled up at me. "Yes, we're not ready for you to come yet." He was obviously enjoying this very much.

Hells, so was I.

I groaned with the effort of keeping an orgasm at bay. With Jake pounding at me from behind, and Cooper slamming into me from below, it took every drop of self-control I had. And a bunch I didn't know I had.

"Please." The word slipped from between my lips before I knew it. If they didn't let me come soon I was going to cry or burst. Or something. Shit was gonna get messy.

"Should we let her?" Cooper asked. Apparently he was a nicer guy than Jake. "Or we could make her last a bit longer." Or he wasn't.

Jake chuckled. "A little bit longer."

"Assholes," I told them.

As if that was somehow an invitation, they both ground into me harder than before. Faster. Deeper. I wanted to scream.

"Okay," Jake said after another minute or two. "You can come now."

I came oh, so, fucking hard I saw stars that were probably from another universe, or some shit. I didn't care. I rode the wave to the peak and screamed my throat raw as my blood thundered through my body.

Both guys came at almost the same time, a few seconds after me. The whole world became a chorus of grunts, groans and panting. Sweat, cum and racing pulses.

The high was so delicious, it took time to come down from. That was fine with me. I could have stayed lost in it for days. Weeks. Forever.

We sagged down onto the bed together and

panted, spent and messy in the most perfect way imaginable.

15

BEN STUCK his head into the bar manager's office on the first floor. "Boss, there's a couple of cops here to talk to you." The expression on his face clearly said what he thought of that. If it was up to him, he wouldn't let them in. Truthfully, that would have been my preference too, but it was easier to deal with them and their suspicions than to brush them off and have them sniff around later.

I nodded. "Show them in." I wished they would call ahead so I could wear something more… distracting, but a deep red, silk blouse with a plunging neckline, and a black skirt with a slit halfway up my thigh, would have to do. Yeah, sometimes I wear colours other than white, and this outfit would make most guys' eyes pop out.

The male cop who stepped inside was evidence of this, but of course his partner was a woman. She had that 'I am not going to be so easy to impress' expression on her face. So many people looked like that when they first met me. Like the rest of them, she would learn.

"I am Detective Ian Gilbert, and this is Detective Fiona Singh." He was at least in his fifties, with salt-and-pepper hair and faded blue eyes. To his credit, he tried to keep his eyes on my face. Every so often, they would want to down to my cleavage and linger there for a few moments.

"We'd like to ask you some questions," Singh said. Her gaze was firmly fixed on my face, eyes narrowed like she thought she knew what I was up to.

She didn't have a fucking clue.

"Of course." I rose and shook both of their hands, but took just a *little* bit longer with Gilbert.

His cheeks flushed.

"Please, take a seat." I sat and waved toward the chairs on the other side of the desk. "Whatever you need, I'll help as much as I can." And if I couldn't, I could always help them to the bottom of the harbour.

"You were a witness to an explosion." Singh crossed her arms over her chest.

I kept my expression icy calm. No wonder they struggled to solve cases. That was three fucking days ago. If I could, I would laugh.

Instead, I sighed. "I was near the newspaper stand when it blew up. It was terrible. I've never seen anything like it." Not on *that* day. I've witnessed plenty of carnage in my time. This one barely rated a mention.

"Why have you not come forward to give us a statement?" Singh asked.

I feigned ignorance. "Oh. Was I supposed to?" And say what, exactly? The stand was collateral damage in a pack war? They wouldn't buy it, even though it was true.

"You want to help us find out who did it, don't you?" Gilbert asked. He was obviously trying to appeal to my sense of justice, but he wasn't going to achieve it by talking to me like I was a kid.

I gaped at him. "You mean it wasn't an accident?" Like hells it was. I put a hand over my mouth. "How awful. Why would anyone do that?"

Because Alistair Dagen was a motherfucking piece of shit, that's why.

"That's what we'd like to find out," Singh said. "We're trying to get to the bottom of it. That's why we need statements from everyone involved."

"Involved?" My eyes widened. "You don't think I have something to do with it?" I looked toward Gilbert as though pleading with him to believe me.

"No," Gilbert said quickly, his hand outstretched toward me. "But we need to find out who was. You want to help with that? Right?"

I wanted to stab him in the eyeball with a fork if he kept being so condescending.

"Of course I do," I said honestly. "All those poor people. They deserve the truth. Their families must be beside themselves wondering what happened. And why." I thought back to the hours, days after my parents were murdered. I thought I knew the answer to those questions, but the more time passed, the more I realised the situation was much more complex. It was about so much more than just my parents. Power struggles were rarely about individuals. People like me just got caught up in them.

"Did you see anyone acting suspicious in the area?" Gilbert asked.

I thought for a moment. "No, not that I can think of. I mean, no more shady than usual. This is Sydney, after all."

Gilbert chuckled. "Yeah, it is."

Singh gave him a dark look. She gave me the

impression she didn't like him very much. Tough shit, that was her problem.

She looked back at me. "Why did you not stay in the area until the police arrived? Or render assistance to those who were injured?"

"Honestly?" I sighed. "I panicked. The newspaper stand exploded and I was knocked off my feet. People were crying. Other people looked dead. It was scary. I didn't think I was badly hurt enough to need an ambulance, so I thought I should get out of the way." I turned my best puppy dog eyes on Gilbert. "You just said it wasn't an accident. What if it happened again? The safest place to be was away from there."

Gilbert nodded his understanding.

I should get an acting award for this shit.

Singh was not so easy to convince. "So you ran?"

"Staggered," I replied. "My ears were ringing and my balance wasn't quite right."

I sat back in my chair and decided to level with her. "The fact you're here would suggest that people were able to identify me on sight. That would be because I am what the media would refer to as a rich nightclub owner. Whenever anything goes down, we're the first to have fingers pointed at us."

I sat forward and propped my elbows on the

desk. "Everything we do here at Crimson is legal and transparent. We pay taxes, we pay our staff above minimum wage. Our hygiene standards are above minimum requirements. If there is even a sniff of drugs, the customer is not allowed in, or is kicked out. You will have records of the police being contacted on those occasions." Only because it helped us to look like we were above board. And because I hated drugs. Keep that shit out of my properties if you like being alive and with functioning knees.

Singh nodded that that was indeed true. Obviously she looked into my background before she came.

I went on. "The very fact that Crimson is all about sex means people are happy to assume the worst about me and those who work with me. That doesn't mean I went around blowing up any newspaper stands. In fact, I only went there to buy a bag of jelly beans." I spread my hands.

"Some would suggest that fleeing the scene of the crime would imply guilt," Singh said. She really wasn't letting up, was she? What a pain in the ass.

"Others would suggest that somebody who is as easily identifiable as I am would be pretty fucking stupid to blow up a newspaper stand with myself standing really close to it," I said. "I don't have a death wish."

"Do you have any enemies?" Singh asked.

I held back a snort. Did I ever?

"There's a long list," I said. "It starts with any number of conservative politicians and ends with people whose partners prefer to be here than at home." I frowned. "You think this was aimed at me?"

"Do you?" Singh asked.

"I think I ducked down the street to get a bag of jelly beans and got caught up in some shit that happened to go down when I was there," I said. "Why blow that up if they were after me? It's not like I go down there every day. They might have been after someone else in the area. Or whoever owned the place." I shrugged. "Not to tell you how to do your job or anything." I smiled sweetly and not at all sincerely.

Gilbert smiled back, but Singh grunted.

"If anything else like this happens, contact us," she said. "Having to track you down took time and resources we can't afford to waste."

Yeah, she probably asked someone on the street.

"I'm sorry," I said. "I didn't mean to cause any inconvenience. I really didn't hear anything or see anything out of place." That was sincere, I really hadn't. The most suspicious things I saw were Jake, Cooper, Ben and me. Luckily for us, being ridiculously attractive wasn't a crime.

Gilbert nodded and stood. "If you think of anything, please contact me. Us." He cleared his throat.

Singh rolled her eyes and then tried to look like she hadn't. She had a lot of work to do if she ever wanted to become an actor.

Just for shits and giggles, I rose and leaned forward to shake Gilbert's hand again, giving him a nice eyeful of cleavage.

He stared and gulped, then managed to shake my hand. "Thank you for your time." His voice was an octave or two higher than before.

"You're welcome," I said smoothly. I took back my hand and offered it to Singh.

She gazed at it and turned and walked out the door. Gilbert looked apologetic, then followed, just as Jake stepped inside.

He closed the door behind him. "It's always a good day when you get a visit from the po-po."

I sank back into my chair and snorted. "Waste of fucking time." I told him about the conversation. "Can you believe they actually thought I would try to blow myself up?"

Jake chuckled and shook his head. He pulled a lollipop out of his pocket, then apparently thought twice and put it back.

"Did you enlighten them?"

"What would be the point?" I asked. "Gilbert was only here to get his cock sucked. Or because Singh made him come. She was only here to further her career. You know the type. She sniffs around until she finds something on me, just so she can collect the accolade for bringing me down." She wasn't the first. She would be the last. They were an annoyance, but little more than that. She would disappear if she became a problem. Gilbert could be bribed or black-mailed. I would prefer to deal with two of him than one of her any day.

"Do you want her dead?" Jake asked lightly.

I rubbed my forehead. A headache was starting to threaten my temples. "No. If she disappears now it will be too obvious. Even an—"

My head jerked up. "Shit. Have someone keep an eye on her. This is exactly the kind of crap Dagen will be looking out for. She dies, it gets pinned on me. I don't need that kind of bullshit right now." Or ever.

Jake nodded then rose and came around behind

me. He placed his hands on my shoulders and started to massage them.

"You know they would never make it stick."

"I know, but I don't need the publicity. It's bad for business." And I didn't want to be locked away in a cell for any length of time.

I closed my eyes and enjoyed the feeling of his hands smoothing out my knotted muscles.

"Maybe it would be easier to kill her on our terms," Jake said. "We can make it look like an accident. Dagen will make it look like the murder it really is."

"I'm not sure if you're saying that because it's a good point, or just because you would like to kill someone," I said.

He chuckled. "A bit of both? If she is going to create trouble for you, then it will be a pleasure. And if Alistair Dagen is going to use her to create even more trouble, then even better."

"Unless this is exactly what he wants us to do," I said. "In which case he'll make sure someone sees the accident. Fuck." My headache was getting worse.

"He's getting very good at getting into your head," Jake said. "You should start charging him rent."

"Oh, I am," I replied. "It accumulates every time I think about him. As it stands, his great-great grandchildren will inherit the debt." I grimaced at the idea of him reproducing. I didn't doubt he had, but he was smart enough to keep that information from me.

The door opened and closed. I opened my eyes long enough to see Cooper enter and flop down in a chair.

"I saw the cops outside just now." His ridiculously gorgeous face creased in a frown. "They asked about my uncle. I told them he was out of the country for work, but I don't think they bought it."

"Fucking hells," I muttered. "You better make her and Gilbert have a nasty accident. And figure out who at the station is letting them sniff around. I pay them well enough, I shouldn't have to deal with this."

"My guess is an anonymous tip," Jake said. "I'll talk to our people down there, but you know how it is. Sometimes they have to pretend to look into us."

"It didn't seem like pretend to me," Cooper said. He squirmed in his seat.

"You weren't even there," I pointed out. "Don't worry, we'll deal with it. I've already created a paper trail that will lead straight to Dagen. Our purchase of the garage was totally legal. Dagen's dealing with Silas was not. At least, that's what it will show."

Cooper grinned. "Just when I think you couldn't get more awesome, you get more awesomer."

Jake stopped kneading my shoulders for a moment. "Is that a word?"

"I dunno." Cooper shrugged. "It is now."

"It fits me," I said. "But don't get too excited, you haven't seen how much paperwork you have to fill out to start assassin training."

Cooper's expression dropped. "Really? That much?"

I let him stew for a moment, then smiled. "No. Of course not. What self-respecting assassin would leave evidence like that around for people to find?"

Cooper's grin was back. "Great, because I hate filling out forms. It makes me stabby."

"What doesn't make you stabby, Murder Pup?" Jake asked.

"Ivory," Cooper replied. He looked sly before adding, "Unless you're talking about stabbing my cock into her pussy. Then I'm definitely stabby. A lot."

"You and me both, Pup," Jake said. "You and me both." He kissed the top of my head.

"She does have that effect on people, doesn't she?" Cooper sighed and gave me a look that made my heart do a flip in my chest like a gymnast.

I adored both guys in different ways but to the same extent. I had known Jake for practically a lifetime, and Cooper for the blink of an eye, but I couldn't imagine my life without either one of them. I couldn't even bring myself to think the L-word, I was so scared of what would happen if I did.

Love made you vulnerable. It was a distraction, potentially a dangerous one. It could get you hurt. But fuck, I felt what I felt.

"Don't you two have a former nightclub owner to dispense with?" I asked.

"Haigwood," Jake said. "Yes we do." He turned my face to kiss my mouth, then drew back and gave me a look almost identical to Cooper's.

He straightened up. "Come on, Pup." He started toward the door.

Cooper rose, leaned over the desk, put his hands on my upper arms and pulled me to my feet. He drew me closer, kissed my mouth firmly, then let me go.

"Coming." He flashed me a panty melting smile and started after Jake.

"I think I'm going to go home for a while," I said. "I need a break from this place. And some more clothes."

Jake hesitated halfway out the door and frowned. "I could come with you—"

I waved him out. "I'll be fine. I'll just duck over there and come back. I'll take Ben with me. Maybe give him a blow job while we're there," I said teasingly.

Jake groaned. "Lucky him."

Neither guy had a hint of annoyance or anything on their faces other than envy for Ben.

"Go do your jobs," I scolded. "I'll see you both later."

Cooper blew me a kiss. "Later."

Jake pulled out the lollipop, took off the wrapper and grinned at me before he shoved it into his mouth.

I shook my head at him. "Go." Before I changed my mind and kept them here to fuck their brains out. Or took the lollipop and ate it myself.

"Okay, okay, we're going," Jake said. He turned to winked at me, then closed the door behind him.

16

"DID you know Jake gives me shit because all my cars have manual transmission?" I asked. I stopped my little white Cobra at the lights and glanced over at Ben. He didn't look any worse for wear having survived the explosion. He looked more worried about surviving my driving. I would show him I was a good driver.

He chuckled. "He might have mentioned it a time or two. I know for a fact at least two of his are also manuals."

"The ones he keeps as collectors items." I nodded. "But the rest are automatic." He preferred to drive an oversized truck or SUV. I liked classic, dainty cars and I hated the idea of them sitting in a garage gathering dust.

"According to him," I continued, "I just like to keep my hand on the stick." I smiled over at Ben who chuckled again.

"There's nothing wrong with that," he said. "Plenty of people say they make better cars."

"Exactly," I said. "I knew you'd be on my side."

"Every time," Ben agreed. "Boss." He added after a moment.

"If you disagreed with me, would you say so?" I asked.

"No, boss," he said. A smile tugged at the corners of his mouth. He had ways of letting me know what he was thinking without coming out and saying so. And we both knew it. He'd been working with me long enough.

"What would you do if I asked you to do something you didn't want to do?" I asked.

"I would do it anyway," he said. "Are you planning on doing that?"

"Not planning on it, no. But the night is young." Not really. It was edging eleven p.m. by now. That was early for us though, I supposed.

"I look forward to anything you might ask me to do," he said smoothly, and with more than a little hint of husky desire.

"Are you flirting with me?" I asked. When the

light turned green, I put the Cobra into gear and floored it.

Ben jerked back against the seat. "Do you want me to flirt with you?"

"I don't know. I'll have to think about that one. I'll let you know." I wound around a delivery truck and headed toward William Street. That would take us east toward Point Piper. No road in Sydney got you anywhere quickly these days, but this was the fastest way home. On a good day, that was. On a bad day, I wished I took the helicopter home.

"Okay. You know where to find me." I caught a quick flash of his grin in a street light before we headed into heavier traffic.

I glanced up into the rear view mirror. "That black SUV has been following us almost since we left Crimson."

"Yeah. I've been watching it in the side mirror." Ben twisted around to look out the back. "They could be going the same way."

Another SUV, also black, pulled out of a side street right in front of us. It sped up a little, then dropped back so both SUVs were equal distance from us.

"What about that one?" I asked. I wasn't worried. Not yet. Plenty of people drove cars like that, and even more drove erratically. The guy in front of us wouldn't be the first driver to pull out in front of another car and then slow right down.

"Coincidences are like unicorns," Ben said. "They might look good on paper, but they don't actually exist."

"And that's how I know you've been hanging around with me for too long," I said. "You're getting cynical."

"To be fair, I've been cynical for a long time. Growing up around witches will do that to you." He kept glancing back behind us, then ahead again. "I think we need to get off this road."

"I think you're right," I agreed. If the two SUVs were just driven by random Sydneysiders, then we would lose them. If not, then we would know they were there for us.

"Hold on." The SUV in front of us slowed down as the light turned orange, but I swerved and wove around him. We shot through the lights just as it turned red.

With apparently no regard for anyone else in the road, both SUVs followed us. They certainly drove like they were evil.

"Okay. That answers that question." Unfortunately, neither one hit another car on the way through. Worse luck.

"Shit, look out," Ben called out as a third SUV pulled out of the street in front of us.

I managed to break hard enough to avoid running into the back of it, but like the last one it sat right in front of us. One of the others pulled up beside us, leaving the last one to follow.

"I'm a wolf, not a cat, but I know boxes have four sides," I remarked. I peered through the windscreen.

"Up ahead," Ben said. "There are two cars before it."

"I see it," I said. I had two options, let us get boxed in or swerve into oncoming traffic.

I took the third option. I braked hard and swerved into a side street, narrowly missing a white delivery van.

"There's at least four of them," I reasoned. "We're either going to have to fight, or we're going to have to run."

"Got it, boss," Ben said. How the fuck did he sound so calm? "Let me out here, I'll lead them away. Assholes won't be able to tell one white wolf from another in the dark." Somehow, he had managed to strip off, but leave his seatbelt on. Those were some skills right there. He unclipped his seatbelt now and let it slide back into place.

"I hope you're right," I said. It wouldn't take them long to realise the wolf they were chasing was bigger than the one they were actually after.

My heart pounded like a drum. I pulled the Cobra up on the side of the road and opened the door beside me.

Ben, already in wolf form, bounded across my lap and shot out the door.

I ducked down. With any luck they would think there was only one of us in the car.

Two of the SUVs wove around the Cobra and followed the white wolf up the street.

The other two stopped behind and in front of the Cobra.

I grabbed up my phone and hit a button on the screen. After a moment or two, Jake's voice came through the speaker.

"Hey." He sounded calm, but he knew this number. Not just that it was me, but that this was one I would only use during an emergency.

"Jake." I tried to keep my voice from wavering. "I need you to do something for me."

He obviously caught the tone in my voice. "El? What's wrong? Where are you?"

"Everything is under control," I lied. "But I need you to do something for me. I need you to call in a favour."

Four forms got out of the SUV in front of me. I looked in the rear view mirror and saw another four.

Fuck.

I quickly told him what I needed him to do.

"Okay, but tell me where you are. What the fuck is going on?" He sounded frantic.

The forms got closer. Not surprisingly, they were all men in black suits. Dagen's men.

I swallowed. "Just… Do what I asked. *Please.*"

"El," he said insistently.

"Jake. I love you." I sucked in a deep breath.

"Elodie, I love you too." He sounded confused.

"Bye," I told him.

"No. Wait. Elodie. *Elodie!*" My name tore out of his throat like something between a shout and a sob.

I ended the call and tossed the phone onto the floor of the car. I took off my watch and threw it down on top of it.

I flicked off my seatbelt. There wasn't time to strip, or to even give a shit about ruining another set of clothes.

I half closed my eyes and shifted into my magnificent white wolf form. Silk and cotton tore to shreds. Buttons popped loose and went flying. I shook the fabric loose and bounded out of the car.

Dagen's men had already started to strip and shift before I bolted past them and headed in the opposite direction from the way Ben went.

I was smaller than the black wolves, which made me more agile, but they were faster. And there were eight of them.

I ducked between parked cars and looked for somewhere, anywhere I could fit that they couldn't follow. Anything to give me even a minute or two head start on them.

I stuck to the shadows, but being white, I had the distinct disadvantage of standing out, even at night.

In wolf form, the smells of the city were stronger, more pungent. Fumes from cars, rubbish and the stink of black wolf.

They would smell me too.

I slowed down to squeeze under a broken fence. I shook and slinked across a used car lot. None of the cars parked in there would have keys in, even if I did have time to check. Worse luck. Another car would be handy right about now. Especially since the black wolves were squeezing under the gate, one by one.

They glided after me like shadows of night.

If I could hide my scent, I would slink under a car

and wait them out. I couldn't. If I did that now, they would pin me down.

How the fuck was I going to get them off my tail?

I bolted towards the road and along the sidewalk. It was way too open here. Fuck.

I loped along the ground as fast as I could push myself. And then a little bit more. I didn't need to look over my shoulder to know they were gaining on me. I could hear them and smell them. They made no attempt to hide their presence. They didn't need to. They knew they had me outnumbered.

I just had to outsmart them.

No pressure.

I headed up the steps to an overpass which stretched across the road. It stank of urine and fresh paint. The local council had recently tried to cover graffiti, by the look of it. And by the look of the new graffiti, they weren't successful for long.

I bolted across the overpass and down the stairs on the other side.

When I was sure the black wolves were following me, I darted across the road to the first set of stairs and headed back the way we all came. With any luck, my scent would be masked by theirs.

They followed me back across the road and narrowly avoided being hit by a passing car.

Crap, that would have helped to thin the pack a little bit.

A glance over my shoulder showed me they weren't fooled by my little trick. If anything, they were closer now. Too close for me to risk squeezing under another gate. I could practically feel their breath on my hindquarters.

Hoping I was heading the right way, I bolted down the street and around the corner. I managed a burst of speed to put some distance between me and my pursuers.

I ran across another road and ducked behind a row of bushes and into an alleyway. I sprinted through there and out the other side. If I calculated correctly I should be one street over from where I was trying to go.

I followed the sidewalk and almost skidded around a bend.

If I could just get far enough ahead…

I bolted past the traffic lights Ben and I stopped at. It seemed like days ago now. It couldn't have been more than twenty minutes.

I flew across the road and into the side street, my heart in my throat. Usually I loved to run in wolf form, but this was bullshit. There was nothing fun about this. Not at all.

My heart rose when I saw my car still parked by the side of the road. It sank again when I saw it was surrounded by several black shadows.

Fuck.

My hesitation was all it took. One of the wolves behind me leapt. He grabbed onto my hind leg with his teeth.

I yelped and scrambled to get away, but his jaw locked down tighter. I felt a snap and crunch of bone.

Shining blood stained my fur.

Instinctively, I kicked for everything I had, but another black wolf grabbed onto another of my legs. Lighter than the first, but firm enough to keep me in place.

Yet another wolf jumped at me and pushed me off my feet. He wrapped his jaws around my throat. His teeth pressed lightly. Not hard enough to do damage, but hard enough for me to get the message.

I took it. I did what any sensible wolf would do. I lay completely still. I hated myself for doing it, but my choices were that or have my throat ripped out. I didn't want Dagen to get the better of me, but I didn't have a death wish.

I closed my eyes and tried to ignore the searing

pain in my leg. There was no way in fuck wasn't broken.

I waited. Why wasn't I dead yet?

I got the answer to that a minute or two later, when yet another dark SUV pulled up. To the surprise of no one, Alistair Dagen stepped out. His shoes made a clicking sound as he walked across the road. He had something in his hand but I couldn't tell what it was until he got closer.

He crouched down beside me. The look of triumph on his face was almost too much to bear.

Motherfucker.

"Shift back," he snapped.

I stared back at him, sending thoughts of him dying suddenly. Maybe wishing for a comet to drop out of the sky onto his head.

At a signal from Dagen, the jaws around my throat tightened.

I swallowed. It was harder to do that. Harder to breathe. The adrenaline from the chase gradually seeped away. Despair threatened to replace it.

No, I told myself. *Just because I'm pinned to the road right now, doesn't mean I'm beaten. No way.*

I huffed out my snout and shifted back into person form.

The wolf's jaws were barely off my neck when Dagen snapped something else onto there. A collar?

He leaned down to speak in my ear. "I've always wanted a pet dog. My parents wouldn't let me have one. Just so you know, that collar will prevent you from shifting. Don't try to take it off, it will hurt like hells. Or better yet, try." He patted my bare ass.

I bared my teeth at him.

He ignored me and stood. "Get the bitch into the back of the car."

A couple of his guys had already shifted back into person form. They grabbed me and pulled me to my feet. With my leg mangled as it was, I couldn't have done it by myself anyway.

"Don't call me bitch," I hissed.

With a snap of his wrist, he gave me a stinging backhand across my cheek.

If it wasn't for the guys holding me up, I would have fallen from the blow and the blaze of pain that blossomed across my face.

"Fuck you," I growled.

He struck me again, harder this time. Hard enough that I felt a crack across my cheekbone. I tried, but I couldn't keep from crying out in pain.

"You will learn, bitch," he snarled. "Get her into the fucking car."

They had to half carry me most of the way there, I couldn't support any weight on my leg, and my head spun.

It wasn't until we got almost all the way there, that I finally saw Ben lying on the ground near the tyres. He had a collar around his neck like the one I had and was clearly badly injured, but alive. He looked up at me with regret in his eyes, but I smiled. Nothing he did would have changed any of this. At least he hadn't gotten himself killed.

They pushed me into the back of the car, then picked up Ben and pushed him in after me. He groaned with obvious pain.

The car door closed behind us and the lock audibly clicked into place.

"This is fucked," he whispered.

"Yeah," I agreed. "But we're alive. We need to focus on staying that way, no matter what happens." My leg and face both throbbed with agony, but I clung to the fact they hadn't killed us yet. That meant there was hope. And while there was hope, I was going to find a fucking way out of this.

The engine started and the car pulled away from the side of the road.

I closed my eyes and prayed to any god who would listen that Jake did what I told him to.

If he didn't, I was screwed.

THANK you for reading the first part of Ivory's story. Find out what happens next in Crimson.

If you loved this book, please leave a review and tell your bookish friends. And your non-bookish friends. Who knows, you might convert them to reverse harem. Lol

ABOUT THE AUTHOR

Maggie Alabaster writes reverse harem romance.

She lives in NSW, Australia with one spouse, two daughters, one dog, and countless birds.

Shop direct from Maggie! Store

Sign up for Maggie's newsletter! Sign Up!

Join Maggie's reader group! Join here!

Follow Maggie on Bookbub! Click here to follow me!

Check out Maggie's website- www.maggiealabaster.com

Twisted Ruck

Bad Ruck

Dirty Ruck

Deadly Ruck

Sparrow and the Mafia Kings

Possessive

Ruined

Corrupted

Pucking Dark Hearts

Pucking Hearts Collide

Pucking Forbidden Hearts

Pucking Hardened Hearts

Dusk Bay Demons

Puck Drop

Breakaway

Power Play

Brutal Academy

Book 1 Heartless

Book 2 Cruel

Book 3 Vengeful

Court of Blood and Binding

Book 1 Song of Scent and Magic

Book 2 Crown of Mist and Heat

Book 3 Sword of Balm and Shadow

Book 4 Whisper of Frost and Flame

Dark Masque

Book 1 Bait

Book 2 Prey

Book 3 Trap

Novella A Very Dark Masque Christmas

Saving Abbie

Book 1 Pitch

Book 2 Pound

Book 3 Session

Book 4 Muse

Book 5 Rhythm

Book 6 Encore

Novella Venomous

Saving Abbie books 1-4

Saving Abbie books 4-6 + Venomous

Ruthless Claws

Book 1 Ivory

Book 2 Crimson

Book 3 Elodie

Harmony's Magic

Book 1 Summoned by Fire

Book 2 Summoned by Fate

Book 3 Summoned by Desire

Shifter's Vault

Book 1 Discarded

Book 2 Deceived

Book 3 Disgraced

My Alien Mates

Book 1 Star Warriors

Book 2 Star Defenders

Book 3 Star Protectors

Academy of Modern Magic

Book 1 Digital Magic

Book 2 Virtual Magic

Book 3 Logical Magic

Complete Collection

Summer's Harem

Book 1: Shimmer

Book 2: Glimmer

Book 3: Flicker

Complete collection

Short reads

Taken by the Snowmen

Jingle All the Way

Also by Maggie Alabaster and Erin Yoshikawa

Caught by the Tide

Book 1–Pursued by Shadows

Book 2 Pursued by Darkness

Book 3 Pursued by Monsters